THE GUNSMITH

453

Deadly Heirloom

Books by J.R. Roberts
(Robert J. Randisi)

The Gunsmith series

Lady Gunsmith series

Angel Eyes series

Tracker series

Mountain Jack Pike series

COMING SOON!

The Gunsmith
454 – Into the Fire

For more information visit:
www.SpeakingVolumes.us

THE GUNSMITH

453

Deadly Heirloom

J.R. Roberts

SPEAKING VOLUMES, LLC
NAPLES, FLORIDA
2019

Deadly Heirloom

ISBN 978-1-64540-149-0

Chapter One

When Clint Adams rode into Winslow, Arizona, he immediately knew something was going on. And because he had just arrived, nobody could blame him for the disturbance.

Most of the activity was at a far end of town. He reined in Eclipse in front of a saloon and decided to get a drink before doing anything else. Also, he might be able to get some information.

It was midday, so he was surprised to find the saloon completely empty, except for the bartender.

"Ah, good," the man said, "a customer."

"Beer," Clint said.

"Comin' up."

The bartender set the mug in front of him.

"I just rode in," Clint said. "Looks like some excitement down at the far end of town."

"You could call it that," the bartender said. "It's a hangin'."

"A lynch mob?" Clint asked.

"Naw, naw, it's all legal and proper," the man said.

"Why aren't you down there?"

"Because it don't excite me to watch a man hang," he said. "Not like most of these ghouls in town."

"Well then," Clint said, "I guess you'll have some customers in here when it's all over."

"There are plenty of saloons between here and the gallows," the bartender said. "But I may get some stragglers."

Clint drank half his beer, looked around. The saloon was spacious, with plenty of tables and chairs, a few gaming tables and a piano.

"Yeah," the man said, seeing Clint's glance, "my piano player and my girls are down there, too."

"What's your name?" Clint asked.

"Bill Jellicoe," the man said. "Folks around here call me Jelly."

"Just the bartender, or owner, too?"

"Owner."

"I didn't see a name over the door."

"It's a saloon," Jelly said. "With gamblin' and girls. Why's it need a name? The saloon Hickok was killed in, just had a number."

Clint didn't like being reminded of his friend's death.

"Passin' through?" Jelly asked him.

"Yeah," Clint said, "these days I'm never really heading anywhere in particular."

"Well, we're usually a nice, peaceful town," Jelly said.

"What's the hanging about?"

"Fella stole a horse."

"Are they still hanging men for horse stealing?" Clint asked. "I thought we'd come a long way from that."

"Well," Jelly said, "he killed the owner to get it."

"Oh."

"Yeah," Jelly said, "horse thief and murderer."

"Did he have a lawyer?"

"Lawyer, trial judge, all legal," Jelly said. He rubbed his big hands over his grey-stubble covered jaw. "I been around sixty years and I never liked hangin's."

"You prefer . . . a firing squad?"

"I don't like executions," Jelly said, "but yeah, shootin's better than hangin'."

"A dentist in Buffalo, New York has come up with a new method," Clint said.

"Yeah? What's that?"

"A chair," Clint said.

"A chair?"

"They put the prisoner in a chair and then they run electricity through his body until he's dead."

"And this is bein' used?"

"No, not yet," Clint said. "I read that they're trying to get it right. It's probably still a few years away from being used."

"So that'd be like gettin' struck by lightning, right?"

"Right."

3

Jelly made a face.

"Still think shootin's better. One bullet in the head. Bang. Dead."

"I think I agree with you," Clint said, "given our three choices."

"Bet you've seen your share of hangin's," Jelly said.

"What makes you say that?"

"You look like a fella's been around, is all," the bartender said. "No offense."

"None taken."

They both heard boot steps on the boardwalk outside.

"Sounds like the festivities might be over," Jelly said.

"I better get going, then," Clint said. "I need a livery and a hotel."

"Try Thompson's livery," Jelly said. "A few blocks, you'll have to pass the gallows to get to it, though."

"Like you said," Clint commented. "I've seen my share of hangings. Another one's not going to shock me."

"Well then, after the livery, keep goin' another block, you'll come to the Wicker Hotel."

"Wicker?"

"That's the name of the feller who owns it," Jelly said, "not what it's made of." He laughed.

"Oh," Clint said, "in that case, I'll try it. Thanks."

"Then come on back here tonight and you might see a pretty girl or a game you like."

"Right after I get something to eat."

"Hey," Jelly called out, as Clint headed for the door, "you like steak?"

Chapter Two

Clint got Eclipse boarded at Thompson's Livery and himself at the Wicker Hotel. He went to his room to drop off his bedroll and saddlebags, then came back down to the lobby. In the short time he had been gone, many people had entered the hotel and were milling about. Some of them he could see were newspapermen, others were guests, and some seemed to be citizens who were being interviewed by the reporters.

Clint went to the front desk and spoke to the young clerk who had checked him in.

"Is this all because of the hanging?" he asked.

"Yes," the clerk said. "Some of the newspapermen have rooms here. The rest of them are just people who came to town to be spectators."

"So, there's nothing like a good hanging, huh?" Clint observed.

"That's how a lot of folks feel, sir," the clerk said, with a shrug.

"And you? Were you at the hanging?"

"Oh, no sir," the clerk answered. "I had to stay here, at work."

"Hmm," Clint said, "too bad."

"Not really," the clerk said. "I didn't want to see it."

"Well, good for you," Clint said. "Can you give me directions to O'Neil's Steakhouse?"

"How do you know about that?" the clerk asked, with a frown.

"I stopped at a saloon when I first rode into town," Clint said. "The bartender, a man named Bill Jellicoe, told me about it."

"Yes, Jelly," the clerk said. "Sir, I assure you, you can get a fine steak right here in our dining room."

Clint turned and looked at the doorway that led to the dining room.

"It seems to be pretty busy in there, what with news-papermen and spectators and guests," he said. "I'll try O'Neil's."

"Very well," the clerk said. "Just go out the door, turn left and walk two blocks. You'll see it."

"Thanks."

He made his way through the lobby, side-stepping groups of people who were discussing the hanging. Some of them were laughing about it. The hanging seemed to have been a very popular event.

Outside he made the left turn and walked two blocks. The streets were empty, because most of the saloons and restaurants he passed were packed with folks celebrating the hanging. As he walked, snippets of conversation came to him, and they were all concerned with the execution.

When he reached O'Neil's, he saw that he might as well have gone into the hotel dining room. The restaurant seemed just as crowded.

He went in anyway.

With the hanging the big attraction in town, he felt pretty certain no one knew who he was. Except the desk clerk, since he'd signed the register with his real name. But the young man really hadn't looked at it, simply handed him a key. Still, when a man in a white apron asked him if he wanted a table, Clint said, "Yes, something in the back."

"No problem," the man said. "Nobody ever wants to sit there.

The man led him to a small back table, with no one in the place paying him any special attention. He started thinking that the hanging might actually benefit him, at least for a little while.

A waiter came over and asked, "What'll ya have?"

"A steak."

"It might take a while," the man said. "We're swamped, what with the hangin', and all. Looks like nobody's eatin' at home, tonight."

"That's all right," Clint said. "I'll just take a pot of coffee while I wait."

"Comin' up."

The waiter had to push through a crowd to get to the kitchen. People were standing in the way, talking to some of the others who were seated, and either eating or waiting for their food.

Clint had been in towns before where there'd been a hanging. He had seen people show interest, laugh, cry, stare at the hanging body, or look away from it. But he didn't recall seeing a celebration of this magnitude. It made him wonder who the prisoner had been, as well as who the man he killed had been.

He had passed the gallows there now, and saw the man swinging. Fifteen or twenty people stood staring, but Clint didn't spend much time looking at the body. Now he was thinking, after his meal, if it was still hanging, maybe he'd go over and have a looksee.

He could also talk to somebody, ask questions, and find out most of the answers he was now seeking.

Just out of curiosity.

Chapter Three

Clint didn't know what the desk clerk at the hotel's problem with O'Neil's was. The steak was perfectly palatable, with all the trimmings, and strong coffee. Maybe he just didn't want to lose the business.

Even more townspeople had come in for supper by the time Clint paid his bill and left. The conversation all around him was still about the hanging. He had learned that a man named Jackson had killed a man named Randall over a horse. Randall had caught Jackson trying to steal the horse, tried to stop him, and was killed in the struggle. Jackson did not give the law any reason for the attempted theft.

When Clint walked back toward his hotel, he passed the gallows, intending to have a look. But Jackson's body had finally been cut down. There were no longer any people crowding around, staring.

Clint continued on, passing the Wicker Hotel—which still appeared as if it was under siege—and on to the saloon. When he entered, he saw the place was half full. Along the way he had seen other saloons seemingly filled to the rafters, so he assumed these were the "stragglers" Jelly had talked about.

Jelly waved at him and had a beer on the bar before Clint got to it.

"Thanks."

He looked around, saw two pretty girls working the floor, but no piano player.

"No piano?" Clint asked.

"He didn't come back," Jelly said. "I think he's off somewhere, still celebrating."

"Are these all your girls?"

"Yeah, I only use two at a time."

Clint saw the covers still on the gaming tables.

"No dealers?"

"They're probably with the piano player," Jelly said. "If they're not back tomorrow, they're fired."

"Nice of you to give them the day off." He looked around again, his back to the bar, this time. "Are these your regulars?"

"Some of 'em," Jelly said. "Did you and your horse get settled in?"

"Both of us, yeah, thanks," Clint said.

"And O'Neils?"

"They were busy, but they managed to fit me in," Clint said.

"Good. Enjoy your beer. I have some other customers."

Jelly moved down the bar, while Clint continued to sip his beer and study the room. One of the girls, a pretty brunette noticed him, served the drinks she was carrying on her tray, and then approached him.

"You're new," she said, standing so close to him he could smell the scent she wore.

"Yes."

"I'm Annie."

"Clint. It's nice to meet you."

"You need another beer," she said. "Can I get it for you?"

"Why not?"

He set his empty on her tray, watched her go to the other end of the bar, where Jelly was. They spoke, Jelly nodded and placed a fresh beer on her tray. She balanced it expertly as she carried it to Clint.

"Here you go, handsome," she said. "I hope you'll do all your drinkin' in town with us."

He took the beer from the tray.

"We'll see," he said.

"Well, you tell me if I can do anythin' else to . . . convince you."

She turned and went back to her rounds on the floor.

"She likes you."

He turned and saw Jelly standing at the bar behind him.

"She's doing her job," Clint said.

"You'll see."

Clint drank half the fresh beer down and set the rest on the bar.

"Leavin'?" Jelly asked.

"I was riding all day," Clint said. "I'm going to spend some time in my room and make sure, as you said, that none of the furniture is made from Wicker."

"Come back any time," Jelly said. "I'll have the gaming tables goin' tomorrow."

"I'll check in with you."

Clint left the nameless saloon and walked to the Wicker Hotel. The lobby had emptied out some, but there were still a few newspapermen sitting in chairs, writing as quickly as they could.

When one of them saw Clint enter, he got up and ran to intercept him.

"Excuse me, sir," he said. "Did you see the hanging this afternoon?"

"I didn't," Clint said. "I arrived after it was all over."

"I see," the man said. "Can you tell me what you think—"

"You don't want to know what I think," Clint said, "Excuse me."

He left the man standing there and went up the stairs to his room.

Chapter Four

Clint had two books in his saddlebags, a Dickens and a Mark Twain, but he wasn't up to starting either one of them. Instead, he decided to clean his pistol and rifle, since he had been on the trail a while—including getting stuck in a dust storm in Nevada. He wanted to make sure that both weapons were in perfect working order.

By the time he had broken both down, cleaned them thoroughly, and reassembled them, his eyes were drooping. He made sure his door was locked and checked the window to be certain no one could access the room from there. He saw that he was overlooking the alley that ran alongside the hotel.

When all of that was done, he slipped off his trousers, shirt and socks, got into bed and fell asleep almost immediately.

Not a sound sleep, but as sound as a man like the Gunsmith could safely indulge in.

***

His stomach woke him early the next morning. When he came down to the lobby, he decided to take the clerk's advice from the night before and have breakfast in the hotel dining room.

Ham-and-eggs seemed simple enough, with biscuits and coffee, and it was perfectly edible. He wondered, though, if he would have a truly great meal before he left town? It was something he had begun to search for when he came to a new town. Or a town he hadn't been to in a while.

***

When he stepped outside the hotel, the feeling he'd had when he first rode in the day before was gone. That was probably because the hanging had taken place, and there was no longer that atmosphere that something was about to happen. Also, the festive feeling about the town was gone. People walking the street were tending to their daily chores.

He heard hammering and took a walk to see where the noise was coming from. As he suspected, the gallows were being dismantled by several men with hammers. Only one person was watching, a woman standing on the boardwalk, dressed in black. She looked to be crying.

It was none of his business why she was in tears, but he watched anyway while a man wearing a badge approached her. They spoke briefly, then walked together down the street and entered a building.

Curious, Clint walked down to see what the building was. As he approached, there was a sign above the door that said UNDERTAKER.

Because of the tears and black garb, he assumed the woman was some sort of relation to the dead man, Jackson, wife, or perhaps daughter.

Clint was aware that his natural curiosity had gotten him into trouble in the past, but what's the harm, he wondered? Along with her tears and the way she was dressed, the woman was extremely attractive. He decided to take up a position across the street and wait for her to reappear, just to get a better look at her.

Fifteen minutes later, the sheriff and the woman came out, and they seemed to be in the midst of a terrible argument. She was yelling at him and waving her arms, while the man with the badge seemed to be trying to ward her off. Finally, he just waved his arms and walked away from her.

"Don't walk away from me!" she shouted after him, but he kept going. Rather than chase him, though, she turned and went back inside.

Moments later, a large man in white shirt sleeves forcibly shoved her out the front door.

"You can't do this!" she shouted.

She tried to go back in, but this time the big man grabbed her by her upper arms.

Clint decided he'd seen enough and hurried across the street.

"That's enough," he said. "Let her go!"

The man looked at Clint, and the gun in his holster, released the woman and stepped back.

"Then get her away from here," he said. "She's a crazy woman."

"I'm not crazy," she said, looking at Clint. "This man had stole something from my father."

"Her father's dead," the man said. "They hung him yesterday."

"That's right," she said, "and you've stolen his things."

"I haven't stolen anything," the man said. "I've put his personal effects in a box. It's inside."

"I've seen it," she told Clint. "Something's missing."

"What was it, Miss?"

"My father's pocket watch."

Clint looked at the man he assumed was the undertaker.

"Where's the watch?"

"What watch?" the man asked. "There was no watch."

"He's lying!" she yelled.

"Ask the sheriff," the undertaker said. "He'll tell you. She's crazy."

"I'm not crazy!" she shouted.

"Just keep her away from here!" the undertaker said, and went inside.

"Hey, wait—"

She started to follow him, but Clint stepped in her way.

"Miss," he said, "why don't we go and have a cup of coffee and talk about this? Maybe I can help."

"Why would you want to help?" she asked. "Nobody else from this town does."

"Well," he said, "I'm not from this town."

Chapter Five

They walked a few blocks and found a small café with nothing but empty tables. Clint got his customary back table, away from doorways and windows, and ordered a cup of coffee each. Clint took the time to study the woman seated across from him. She had auburn hair, brown eyes and a full, pouty mouth. Actually, it looked more sulky, but that might've been because of her current mood. In any case, she was a beauty who appeared to be in her early thirties.

"My name is Olivia Jackson," she said. "The man they hung yesterday was my father."

"I'm Clint Adams," he said. "I just rode in moments after that happened."

"I was supposed to meet my father here, but when I arrived, he was already in jail, sentenced to hang. There was nothing I could do to stop it."

"I hope you didn't watch," Clint said.

"I didn't. Afterward, I went to the undertaker and made arrangements. He said he would put my father's personal effects aside for me, but when I looked into the box—"

"—the watch was missing."

"Right."

"And the sheriff believes the undertaker that there was no watch?"

"Yes."

"What's so special about the watch?" he asked.

"Nothing," she said. "It has a picture of my mother inside. That's it."

"Is it gold?"

"I don't believe so."

"If the undertaker did steal it, it has to have some value," Clint said.

"So you don't believe me, either?"

"I didn't say that," Clint said. "I'm just looking for a reason."

She put her cup down.

"I don't know what to do. Apparently, yelling at the undertaker and the sheriff isn't accomplishing anything. Do you think you could help me, Mr. Adams?"

"If you agree to call me Clint," he said. "I'll try."

***

Clint decided they should go and talk to the sheriff.

"I don't know who's worse, him or the undertaker," she confessed. "Or maybe they're in it together."

"Let's go to his office so I can talk to him," Clint said. "What's his name?"

"Sheriff Osborne," she said. "That's all I know."

They left the café and walked to the sheriff's office, entered without knocking. The office appeared to be new, was very clean inside, which is not what Clint was used to seeing. The new, modern police departments, yes, but not a sheriff's office. Even the man with the badge seemed too clean.

"Sheriff Osborne?" Clint asked.

The man looked up from his desk, saw the woman and rolled his eyes.

"Miss Jackson," he said, "I told you—"

"Sheriff," Clint said, cutting the man off, "my name is Clint Adams. Miss Jackson seems to feel that something's been stolen from her father's effects. I was wondering what you were doing about that?"

"Adams," the sheriff said, obviously recognizing the name. He licked his lips and asked, "Why are you involved in this?"

"I saw the undertaker manhandling Miss Jackson, and stepped in. Then she told me her story."

"Yeah, she told me her story, too," the sheriff said.

"And what did you do about it?"

"I talked to him," the lawman said. "He says he never saw a watch."

"There was a watch!" Olivia insisted.

"There might've been, Miss," the sheriff said, "but it looks like it didn't make it to the undertaker's."

Olivia looked at Clint.

"They're lying!"

"In your mind, Sheriff," Clint asked, "there's no chance the undertaker stole it?"

"Abner's been the undertaker here for twenty years," Sheriff Osborne said. "You think he wouldn't last that long if he was a thief."

Clint studied the lawman. He was too young to have also been there for twenty years—at least, as sheriff—but he certainly could've been there for ten or twelve.

"Well," Clint said, "if you don't mind, I'll talk to him myself, just to get a feel for the man."

"Be my guest," Osborne said. "You'll come to the same conclusion I did."

"So," Clint said, "if you're convinced the undertaker didn't take it, what're you doing next?"

"I'll ask around," Osborne said, "see if anybody even saw the watch."

Clint still didn't know what Jackson was doing in Winslow, or how long he had been there. He needed to learn those things from Olivia.

"All right, Sheriff," Clint said, "thanks for your time."

"Sure," Osborne said, "Mr. Adams. Whatever I can do to help."

"Come, Olivia," Clint said, turning for the door.

"That's it?" she asked. "That's all you're gonna do? Take his word—"

"I'm not taking anybody's word for it," Clint said. "We're not finished looking, and I'll probably talk with the sheriff again . . . soon."

Olivia looked at the lawman, saw something pass over his face.

Fear.

Chapter Six

"Wait!"

Olivia grabbed his arm as they were walking away from the sheriff's office, turned him.

"What?"

"He was afraid of you," she said. "Why?"

"He recognized my name."

"Clint Adams?" she asked. "What—who are you?"

"Some call me the Gunsmith," he said. "Have you ever heard that name?"

"Gunsmith," she repeated. "I'm from back East, Clint, I—wait. I remember. Dime novels, right?"

"Right."

"But . . . they're true?"

"Not entirely," he said.

"So then . . . you're some kind of legend?"

"That makes me sound so old," he said. "Let's just call me . . . infamous."

"Then why . . . why would you want to help me?"

"Because you need help," he said.

"It's that simple for you?"

"Usually," he said.

"Maybe you can help me, after all," she said.

"Let's see what the undertaker has to say," he suggested, and they kept walking.

***

The undertaker looked at them as they entered. Clint had seen him just a short time ago, but already the man seemed bigger to him.

"You're back," he said, in a monotone voice.

"We just have a few questions, Mister . . .?"

"Weatherly," the man said, "Abner Weatherly."

"The sheriff tells me you've been the undertaker here for twenty years," Clint said. "You don't look old enough."

"I took over from my father," Weatherly said. "He was forty when he died. I'll be forty next year."

"Well," Clint said, "I'll just take a few minutes of your time."

"Is this still about that watch?" Weatherly said. "I told you—"

"You better tell him the truth," Olivia snapped. "He's the Gunsmith, you know."

"Gunsmith?" Weatherly asked, looking at Clint.

"Clint Adams will do," Clint said.

"Why are you getting involved with this?" Weatherly asked. It was oddly the same question the sheriff had asked.

"The lady needs help," Clint said, "especially when a man as big as you puts his hands on her."

"Look, I—I didn't mean no disrespect," Weatherly said.

"Just give the lady her father's belongings."

"Sure, sure," Weatherly said. "The box is in the back. I'll get it."

He went through a curtained doorway, came back a few moments later. Clint was ready if the man had a gun, but all he had was a partially filled box.

"His clothes, his boots, his gun, his wallet . . . everythin' he had on him, or in his hotel."

"Except his watch!" Olivia snapped.

"Miss," Weatherly said, "if he had a watch, it didn't make it here. Maybe somebody stole it from his hotel room, or from him while he was in jail."

That reminded Clint he still had a lot of questions for Olivia.

Clint took the box from the man.

"Thanks," Clint said. "After we go through this, I'm sure we'll be back with some more questions."

"I don't know what else I can tell you, Mr. Adams," Weatherly said.

"Well, we'll find out, won't we," Clint said.

He went out the door with Olivia.

***

"That was wonderful!" she said, on the street.

"Which way to your hotel?" he asked.

"That way." She pointed.

"What was wonderful?" he asked, as they walked.

"That big man was afraid of you," she said. "He could probably break you in half!"

"I'm sure he could," Clint agreed.

"But he was afraid of you!" she exclaimed. "It must be great to have people be afraid of you."

"I wouldn't say that."

"Well," she said, "you're not a woman in a man's world, are you, Mister Clint Adams?"

"No," he said, "I'm definitely not that."

"You know," she said, "for the first time since I got to town, I'm thinking maybe there's some hope. That's because of you, Clint. Thank you."

"You're welcome," he said, wondering what the hell she was talking about?

Chapter Seven

Her hotel was several streets down from his. It was called THE HOLLAWAY HOUSE HOTEL. Clint had the feeling people in this town named their hotels after themselves.

They walked across the lobby, which was small and empty. Off to the right were a few tables which acted as the hotel's dining room. To the left, batwing doors that led to a saloon, next door.

"Come upstairs," she said.

He carried the box up the stairs behind her, and down the hall to a room. He waited while she unlocked it with a key and then they entered. He put the box on the bed, turned to face her.

"You want to go through this?" he asked.

"Yes," she said, "but I know the watch isn't there."

"Let's go through it, anyway," he said, "and while we do, you can tell me what happened to your father."

"They killed him," she said.

"Yes, well," he said, "I'd like to know what happened, and why he was put on trial and hanged."

"I don't even know that," she said. "I was told he tried to steal a horse, and, while doing that, killed the owner. That doesn't sound like my father at all."

"Well," Clint said, "now I know what other questions to ask the sheriff."

"Good luck," she said. "I tried to get all the facts, but he said I wasn't really entitled to them."

"You're the man's daughter," Clint said. "Who else would be entitled to those facts?"

"He said I wasn't here when it happened, there was really nothing I could do about it, so what was the point?"

"I'll find out what I can," Clint said.

"He won't dare try to brush you off like he did me," she said. "I'm so grateful you've come to my rescue, Clint."

"Let's see how it all goes before you thank me," he said. "Why don't you try to relax for a while? I'll come back and get you later, we'll go to supper, and I'll tell you if I've managed to find out anything."

She approached him, put her arms around him and hugged him tightly. He could feel the solid curves of her body.

"And later tonight," she said, almost into his ear, "I'm going to show you how truly grateful I can be."

He released her before she could feel that his body was reacting to their contact. There was the distinct possibility he wouldn't get out of that room for a long time if he didn't leave right at that moment.

***

When Clint left the hotel, he decided that there was someone he could talk to before going back to the sheriff or the undertaker.

During the course of the morning, he remembered walking past the office of the *Winslow Informer*. He thought he might get the information Olivia wanted from the editor of the newspaper.

He entered the office and was greeted by the familiar clatter of a printing press, and smell of ink. The man at the press didn't see him right away, but, when he did, he waved a black-stained hand and then shut the press off.

"Help ya?" the old timer asked. He wore a dark visor, with patches of gray hair sticking out in all directions.

"I'm looking for the editor," Clint said.

"That'd be Simon," he said.

"Simon who?"

"Simon Cooper," the man said. "He's in the office." He pointed toward the back. There was a door, but no windows. In many newspaper offices, there was a partition with windows so the editor could see everything that was going on.

"Thank you."

Clint walked to the door in the back wall and knocked.

Someone yelled, "Come in!" just before the press started up again.

Clint entered, and a man sitting at a desk that faced a wall turned in his chair to see who was coming into his office.

"Well," the young man said, "A strange face." He stood up. "How can I help you?"

"You're the editor?"

"Editor and reporter," the man said.

"You seem—"

"—young? I am. I'm twenty-two. I took over from my father a year ago. He died of a heart attack."

"I'm sorry."

"Thank you. I thought somebody should keep the paper going, so I took it on. What can I do for you?"

"My name is Clint Adams. I'm—"

"The Gunsmith," the youngster said, "I know. Damn, what a pleasure."

He stuck his hand out and they shook.

"What can I do for you, Mr. Adams?"

"I'm interested in this hanging that took place yesterday," Clint explained.

"Barbaric!" Cooper said.

"Yes," Clint agreed, "but I'm more concerned with why Jackson was sentenced to hang. I mean, I understand he was charged with stealing a horse and killing the owner, but I'd like to know exactly what happened."

"So would I," Simon Cooper said, "but I'll tell you what I know."

Chapter Eight

"The horse was owned by a man named Dizzy Randall."

"What kind of horse?"

"Nothing special," Cooper said. "A five-year-old mare."

"Then why would someone try to steal it?"

"That's what I asked."

"Who did you ask?"

"Mr. Jackson," Cooper said.

"They let you talk to him?"

"They had to," Cooper said. "How else was I going to write anything?"

"And what did Jackson say?"

"He claimed not to have stolen the horse, and not to have killed Randall."

"How did he get convicted?"

"Eyewitness testimony."

"Somebody saw him kill Dizzy Randall?"

"Yes," Cooper said. "and they testified to that fact."

"Here's a thought," Clint said. "Could they have been lying?"

"Well, of course," Cooper said, "but the Judge believed them."

"The Judge?" Clint asked. "No jury?"

"No, the Judge presided, and served as the jury."

"Maybe I should talk to him then," Clint said.

"Why are you getting involved in this, if I may ask?" Cooper said.

"I saw a lady being mistreated and decided to help her."

"Do you do that a lot?" Cooper asked. "Come to the aid of damsels in distress?"

"More than I should," Clint admitted.

"And does it often get you in trouble?"

"More than you know," Clint said. "But I guess I'm just stubborn that way. I see a woman—or anyone—being mistreated, and I have to step in."

"Interesting," Cooper said. "I don't suppose you'd sit with me for an interview, would you?"

"Not a chance," Clint said. "I don't do interviews."

"Right," Cooper said. "I had to ask."

"What's the judge's name?"

"Anderson," Cooper said. "Judge Jedediah Anderson."

"And what's his story?"

"He's been on the bench for at least forty years," Cooper said. "Some say he's way past it."

"Well," Clint said, "this decision might be an example of that."

"You could be right."

"Were you in court?"

"I was."

"And everyone went along with this?"

"Most of them," Cooper said. "But the Judge and Sheriff seemed to push it over the top."

"Did Jackson have a lawyer?"

"No."

"And who prosecuted him?"

"The Sheriff."

"But he's not a lawyer," Clint observed.

"No, he's not."

"So Mr. Jackson didn't get a proper defense."

"No, he didn't," Cooper said.

"And did you write about that in your newspaper?" Clint asked.

"I wanted to," Cooper said, "but I was warned not to."

"By who?"

"The Sheriff."

"Seems to me Jackson got railroaded," Clint said.

"Some people may have thought that," Cooper said, "but nobody said it out loud."

"Well, maybe somebody should. Do the Judge and the Sheriff run this town?"

"I wouldn't say they run the town," Cooper said, "but they're the law."

"Does Osborne have deputies?"

"Not regular ones," Cooper said, "but he can put to-gether a posse when he needs to."

"A posse," Clint asked, "or a gang?"

"Whatever he needs," Cooper said. "I never thought of it as a gang, but he had a bunch of them around those gallows this morning."

"Did he need them?" Clint asked.

"No," Cooper said. "Nobody wanted to stop it, and eventually it became like a . . . a circus. There were even people selling candy to the crowd."

"And now that it's over, everybody goes back to their normal lives?"

"Apparently."

"Except for Olivia Jackson."

"Who?"

"The woman I told you about," Clint said. "Jackson's daughter."

"Victor Jackson," Cooper said. "That was his full name."

"Well, his daughter was supposed to meet him, only when she got here, he had already been tried and sen-tenced."

"Oh, that's bad," Cooper said. "Did she watch him hang?"

"No," Clint said, "She wasn't one of the leering spectators."

"Well, that's good."

"But she's lost her father," Clint said, "and she believes something of his was stolen."

"What's that?"

"A watch," Clint said. "It wasn't among her father's effects. She thinks the undertaker stole it."

"That's possible."

"Why do you say that?"

"Well, the present undertaker's father was a thief."

"How do you know that?"

"My father told me," Cooper said. "They knew each other."

"But just because the father was a thief doesn't mean the son is."

"Well," Cooper said, "my father was a newspaperman, and so am I."

"So you're saying fathers influence their son's choices?" Clint asked.

"That's how it worked with me."

"If your father and his father knew each other, why are you and he so far apart in age?"

"My father met my mother late in life," Cooper said. "He was almost fifty when I was born."

"And your mother?"

"She was much younger," Cooper said, "but died in childbirth."

"Giving birth to you?"

"No," Cooper said, "A second child. I might have had a brother or a sister, but they both died."

"I'm sorry."

"My father went on, but he died of the heart attack I told you about."

"So it's just you?"

Cooper smiled.

"Me, and the Informer," he said.

"Mr. Cooper," Clint asked, "tell me about Dizzy Randall?"

Chapter Nine

"Randall owned and ran the livery stable at the end of Bacon Street."

"Is that where he was killed?"

"Yes."

"And who owns it now?"

"I'm not sure," Cooper said.

"But you think you know?"

"Well . . ."

"Come on, Cooper," Clint said.

Cooper hesitated a moment longer, then said, "I believe the new owner is Judge Anderson."

"Well," Clint said, "that might start to explain things . . ."

***

When he knocked on Olivia's door, she opened it quickly.

"Did you find out anything?" she asked.

"Let's go to supper," he said. "And I'll tell you."

She stepped out and pulled the door closed behind her. Instead of her black dress, she was wearing a blue one. It was simple and covered her from neck to ankles. In between everything was very well proportioned.

As they got to the lobby she asked, "Who have you talked to?"

"I'll tell you after we're seated at a table . . . somewhere."

***

The "somewhere" turned out to be a restaurant a few blocks from Olivia's Hotel, in a better part of town. It was busy, but they managed to secure a table for two in the back, after Clint slipped the man at the door a few dollars.

"Your waiter will be with you in a minute," he said.

"Thanks," Clint said.

A waiter came scurrying over to take their order, recommending the beef stew.

"I'll have that," Olivia said.

"I'll have a steak."

"Yessir."

"And bring a pot of coffee and two cups."

"Yessir. Right away."

Clint waited until the waiter had returned with the coffee and poured them each a cup before he started talking. He told her about his conversation with the newspaper editor.

"It sounds like they railroaded my father," she said, when he was finished.

"That's what I thought."

"But . . . why?"

"For his watch?" he asked.

"That makes no sense."

"Well then, maybe he saw or heard something, he wasn't supposed to."

"Like what?"

"I don't know," Clint said. "I've still got to ask more questions."

"The Sheriff?" she asked.

He nodded, and said, "And the Judge."

"Do you think he'll talk to you?"

"He'll talk to me."

When their supper came, they took some time to make a dent in their hunger before speaking again.

"Did you do anything else?" she asked.

"I went to the livery that Dizzy Randall owned."

"And?"

"At the moment it's locked up," Clint said. "I walked around the building, but didn't see anything but a corral in the back."

"There's got to be something," she said. "Some reason they hung my dad, and some reason his watch is missing."

"We're in total agreement on that, Olivia."

***

After supper Clint walked Olivia back to her hotel. He meant to leave her in the lobby, but she asked, "Can you come up? To talk?"

"For a while," he said.

As they entered her room, she walked to the window. The room overlooked the front of the hotel.

"The street is so quiet now," she said. "Yesterday it was like a damned circus."

She came away from the window.

"My father was the last of my family," she said.

"I'm sorry."

"I'm feeling kind of lonely, and overwhelmed," she said. "I'd like you to hold me for a minute."

"I can do that."

She came into his arms and he held her tightly. Once again, the feel of her body against his caused a reaction that was natural.

Her face was pressed to his chest. She lifted it just enough to move her lips to his neck, then reached up to draw his face down so she could kiss him.

"Olivia," he said, "this is nice, but I don't want to take advantage—"

"You're not," she said, unbuttoning his shirt, "I'm the one taking advantage of you." She slid his shirt off and tossed it aside, ran her hands over his chest. "If you don't mind."

"No," he said, as her hands went to his belt, "I don't mind, at all."

Chapter Ten

"The Judge will see you now," the clerk said. His name was Samuel Kipness, a man in his thirties who actually looked like what he was, a legal clerk.

"Thanks, Sam," Sheriff Osborne said, and went into the judge's chambers.

Judge Jedediah Anderson looked up from the papers on his desk as the lawman entered. When he saw who it was, he removed his wire-framed glasses, set them down, rubbed his deep set eyes briefly, ran his hands over his wrinkled face before looking at Osborne again. The Judge's eyes were such a shade of light blue, they were almost opaque.

"Sheriff," he said, "what can I do for you today?"

"I thought you should know," Osborne said, "Clint Adams is in town."

"The Gunsmith?" Anderson said, sitting back in his chair. "What's he doin' here?"

"I don't know why he came here," Osborne said, "but now that he is, he's askin' questions about Victor Jackson."

"Who?"

"The man we hung yesterday mornin'."

"Oh, him," the Judge said. "Why in the world is the Gunsmith interested in him?"

"He's not," Osborne said. "He's interested in his daughter."

"Is that girl still here?"

"Did you think she'd leave before buryin' her father?" the lawman asked.

"She would if you ran her out of town," Anderson said.

"She'll just go to the next town and tell her story."

"We can't have her do that."

"Then we should let her bury him," the Sheriff said.

"And when will she do that?" the judge asked.

"Well, not today," Osborne said. "She and Adams are lookin' for that watch."

"That damn watch again?"

"That's what this is all about, right?"

"This was about murder," Anderson said. "Remember that, will you?"

"Yessir."

"Is Adams going to come to see me?"

"At some point."

"Then when he's ready," Anderson said, "you bring him."

"Yes, sir."

"And keep your eyes on him and this girl," Anderson said.

"Will do."

"It would be wonderful if Adams did something that warranted you running him out of town."

"Me?" Osborne swallowed hard.

"You and some of your deputies," the judge corrected himself.

"Uh, yessir."

"Just keep me informed along the way, Sheriff," Judge Anderson said. "That's all."

"Yes, sir," Osborne said again, and left the judge's chambers.

***

After Osborne was gone, the judge went to the door and yelled, "Samuel!"

Kipness came running in even before the judge got back to his desk.

"Yes, your Honor."

"Get me a short list of men who would fit the job of sheriff," Anderson said.

"Has Osborne quit, sir?"

"No," Anderson said, "he hasn't quit, but we might still need a replacement . . . soon."

Chapter Eleven

It didn't take long for them to get into the bed together, naked.

Olivia's clothes had only hinted at the body beneath them. But the couple of times she'd been in his arms, Clint had felt the curves. Now that she was totally naked, it was easy to see she had solid breasts and hips, and a lovely, curved bottom. Her skin was soft and supple as he ran his hands over her, and she moaned appreciatively when he slid one hand between her legs and probed the tawny forest there.

He found her slick and hot as he slipped one finger inside of her. She gasped and raised her hips and gasped again as he started to kiss her breasts and bite at her nipples.

When she could no longer just lie there and let him have his way, she squirmed about until she got him down on his back, and then she began to return the favor. She kissed his neck, his chest, tongued his nipples, then licked her way down over his belly until she found his hard cock, throbbing and waiting for her attention.

First, she licked the length of it, up one side and down the other, then swirled her tongue around the swollen head before taking it into her mouth.

Clint stretched his body out, reached up to grip the bed rail and gave himself up to the sensations her lips and mouth were causing as she slid him in and out of her hot mouth.

At the same time, she ran her fingers over his legs, scraping her nails over the tender flesh of his inner thighs. She didn't do it hard enough to cause pain, but just enough to make him shudder.

She suckled him until he was almost bursting, then released him, climbed up on top and took his hard cock into her steaming hot pussy.

"Ahhhh," she groaned, settling down on him, "this is what I really needed."

"Then take your time," he told her, gripping her hips, "enjoy it."

"And you?" she asked, smiling down at him.

"Oh," he said, "don't worry. I'll enjoy it."

"Good."

She began to move then, slowly rocking back and forth on him, keeping him inside.

"Oh yeah," she said, her tone breathy, "this is what I needed, all right. Mmmm." She closed her eyes as she continued to move her hips and then, little by little, began to build up her speed.

She changed her position then, choosing to lean over him, placing her hands on his abdomen, and then started moving up and down, rather than rocking back and forth.

She tried to speak, but all that came out was, "Uhn, uhn, oh, uhn . . ." over and over again.

Clint began to move his hips in unison with her, lifting them up off the bed to meet her downward thrusts. The bed began to bounce up and down. He hoped nobody below them would come up to see what was going on.

Finally, she prostrated herself on him, pressing her breasts to his chest. He felt the tremors run through her body, and then she made a high, keening sound, which he assumed she was doing instead of screaming out her pleasure . . .

***

"You didn't finish," she said, later.

"No."

"I'm sorry," she said, "I couldn't hold back, anymore."

"No problem," he said. "This was supposed to be for you, wasn't it?"

She looked down at his body and saw that his cock was still at full mast, hard and long. She reached out and stroked it.

"Poor you . . ." she cooed.

"Keep that up," he said, "and I will finish."

She giggled and said, "I have a better idea."

She shimmied down between his legs, took him into her mouth and began to suck. As he glided in and out of her mouth, he felt the release building and, once again, reached up to grip the bed rail. When he finally exploded into her mouth, he did so with a loud roar . . .

***

After she had released him from her mouth, she once again laid down beside him, and they stayed that way for quite a while, catching their breath.

When he finally decided to move, he felt so weak he would have sworn he was filled with jelly, especially his legs.

"Wow," he said.

"That's what I was thinking," she said. She rolled over to face him, kissed his shoulder. "I have to thank you. You took my mind off . . . things."

"Well, I have to tell you, it was my pleasure," he said. "If you need to get your mind off things again, just let me know."

"Do you mean in the next day or two," she asked, "or, like, the next hour or so?"

He turned to look at her impish smile and said, "Take your pick."

Chapter Twelve

Clint decided to leave Olivia's hotel and not spend the night. He didn't feel comfortable in the room that overlooked the front street and had a balcony outside the window. By now, it was known that he was in town. He didn't want to make it easy for anyone to take a shot at him.

"Will I see you tomorrow?" she asked, before he left.

"Oh yes," he said, "we're not done . . . with any of this."

That pleased her.

He spent the night in his own room, had breakfast in the hotel dining room. His plan for the day was to talk with the judge, see what he could find out about the charges against Olivia's father. But he thought he would check in first with the sheriff, just to let the man know he wasn't going anywhere, anytime soon.

***

Sheriff Osborne looked up at him as he entered the man's office.

"Somethin' I can do for you, Adams?" the man asked.

Olivia had been right, the man was afraid of him, but he was trying to act like he wasn't.

"I just wanted to check in with you, see if you've found out anything about that watch."

Osborne sighed.

"All I've found out indicates that there never was a watch," he said.

"That's ridiculous," Clint said. "Olivia is the man's daughter. She should know if he owned a watch or not."

"Maybe he lost it," Osborne said, "before she got here. Maybe before he even got here."

"No," Clint said, "there was a watch."

"What makes you think so?"

"Because too damn many people are saying that there wasn't."

He turned to leave.

"Where are you going?" Osborne said.

"I think it's time for me to talk to the Judge," Clint replied.

"He won't see you without an appointment."

"He'll see me."

Osborne stood.

"You're right," he said, coming around from behind his desk, "he will . . . if I take you there."

"Then let's go!"

***

The judge's clerk looked up at them as they entered and frowned. Clint didn't know if he was unhappy to see the sheriff, or him, or both.

"Sam, my boy," the sheriff said, "this is Clint Adams. He'd like to see the Judge."

"Does he have an appointment?"

"I don't think he'll need one," Osborne said. "Just tell the Judge he's here."

"This is very irregular."

"Judge Anderson won't be very happy with you if you don't tell him."

The clerk stared at Osborne for a long moment, then stood up, knocked on the door to the Judge's chamber and entered.

"He doesn't like you," Clint said.

"That makes us even," Osborne said.

The door opened and the clerk reappeared.

"Mr. Adams can go in," he said, grudgingly.

"Thank you, Samuel," Osborne said. He turned to Clint and said, "I'll wait here."

"Sure."

"The Gunsmith, I presume," Judge Anderson said.

Clint stared at the man. He looked like someone who had been on the bench for forty years, as he'd been told. His scalp showed pink through his sparse white hair. There was more hair above his eyes than on his head.

"Just Clint Adams will do," Clint said.

"Well then, Mr. Adams, have a seat and tell me what's on your mind."

The only judge Clint had ever met that he had the slightest respect for was Judge Isaac Parker, the hanging judge in Fort Smith, Kansas, even though they didn't like each other.

He didn't expect this man to change his mind about judges, in general.

"Victor Jackson," Clint said.

"Who?"

"The man you hung yesterday," Clint said, then added, "for no reason."

"If I hang a man, Mr. Adams," the Judge said, "there's always a good reason for it."

"So what was the reason for this one?" Clint asked. "A horse? A murder? Or a watch?"

"I'm sorry . . . a watch?"

"You don't play dumb very well, Judge," Clint said. "Mr. Jackson's pocket watch is missing. Inside it was a picture of his wife."

"According to who?" he asked.

"His daughter."

"Who arrived in town almost after the fact."

"I'm sure if she'd known you were planning on hanging her father, she would have shown up sooner."

"All I'm saying is," the Judge went on, "she has no idea whether or not her father lost the watch before he even got here."

"According to her, it was precious to him and he never would have lost it."

"Well," Judge Anderson said, "I'm sure the sheriff is doing his best to find it."

"I don't know that his best will be good enough," Clint commented.

"Hmm," Anderson said, "you may be right. He's not the smartest man in town. But then, he wasn't elected because of his talent as a detective."

"I'm sure he wasn't."

"Perhaps what I should do," the Judge said, "is assign a special investigator."

"Do you have someone in town you could give that job to?" Clint asked.

The Judge looked him right in the eye and said, "I believe I do."

Chapter Thirteen

"Now wait a minute—"

"Don't try to tell me you're not qualified," the Judge said.

"I'm saying I didn't come to Winslow to wear a badge."

"There's no badge involved," the Judge said. "You would have no standing as a lawman. You would simply be tasked with solving the problem of the missing watch."

Clint studied the man for a few moments.

"Are you being serious?" he asked, then.

"Deadly."

"What about the sheriff?"

"He'll assist you in any way he can," Anderson said. "But the job of discovering what happened to that watch would be yours."

"And how would people know about this appointment?" Clint asked.

"My clerk will type up an order," Anderson said, "and we'll have the newspaper print a facsimile of it on the front page. I'm sure the *Informer* would love a headline like THE GUNSMITH APPOINTED SPECIAL INVESTIGATOR."

"I don't think it needs to be in the newspaper."

"And why not?" Anderson asked. "Wouldn't you like everyone to know of your appointment?"

"Actually, no," Clint said, "and neither would you."

"And why not, pray tell?"

"Because if you put a headline like that out, every would-be gunhand in the country would flock to Winslow just for a chance to try me."

"Indeed," the Judge said, thoughtfully, "that might be the case."

"You'd have shootings in the streets, Judge," Clint said. "Innocent people would get hurt."

"All right, then," the Judge said, "what would you prefer?"

"I'd prefer no such appointment."

"You're too late," the Judge said. "I'm entering it into the record."

"And if I refuse?"

"I'll hold you in contempt and have the sheriff toss you into a cell."

Clint studied the man, again.

"And rest assured," the Judge said, before Clint could say a word, "I'll do it."

Clint frowned.

"Do you accept?" Anderson asked.

"You're not exactly leaving me any choice, are you?" Clint asked.

"No."

"All right," Clint said, "you win."

"I don't win, Mr. Adams," Judge Anderson said. "You do. You're getting what you want, somebody to look for that watch. Now, please ask my clerk to step in . . ."

***

They waited while Samuel the clerk typed the order up and brought it in to the Judge.

"Now, I'll sign here," the Judge said, doing so, "and then sheriff, you sign as witness . . ."

Osborne approached the desk, accepted the fountain pen and signed his name.

"And there we have it," Anderson said, holding the piece of paper aloft. "Mr. Adams, you are now a special investigator, reporting to this court."

"Great," Clint said.

"And I had Samuel type up two copies, so you can carry one."

He held it out, and Clint accepted it.

"Show it to anyone in town, and they'll answer your questions."

Clint was feeling frustrated and railroaded. This wasn't what he had in mind, at all, when he came to see the Judge.

Chapter Fourteen

When Clint left, Sheriff Osborne stayed.

"What was the point of that?" the lawman asked.

"Well, for one thing," Anderson said, "he will no longer be on your ass to find that watch. It's his job now."

"Yeah, but . . . why do we want him out there lookin' for that watch?"

"Because," the Judge said, "we're going to make damn sure he doesn't find it."

"And how do we do that?" Osborne said.

"Well first, you're going to help him . . ."

"Am I?"

". . . and get in his way while you do it. And second, get your ass over to the undertaker's and make sure he knows what's at stake."

"Yes, sir."

"Don't mess this up, Osborne," the Judge said.

"No, sir."

Osborne turned and left.

***

Before leaving, Clint turned to the clerk.

"He's a hard man, isn't he?" he asked.

Samuel looked up at Clint.

"He may be hard," he replied, "but he's fair."

"Is he?"

Samuel almost smiled.

"Yes," he said. "Just ask him. He'll tell you that, him-self."

"I'm sure he will."

Clint turned and left.

***

Outside the City Hall building he stopped.

What had just happened?

He had gone in hoping to find out something useful about the man who had sentenced Victor Jackson to hang. Instead, he came out with a piece of paper that put him in charge of finding Victor Jackson's watch.

At first, he thought he should wait for the sheriff to come out, since the judge told him the law would be behind him. But he decided just to proceed on his own, since he now had the authority.

Judge Anderson didn't fool him, though. He gave him the authority, figuring he would never be able to find out anything. And when that happened, he wouldn't be able to blame anyone but himself.

But the Judge had made one mistake. By giving Clint this assignment, he felt the Judge was admitting there was a watch, and somebody had stolen it.

Before he could find the watch, however, Clint had to find out why it had been taken.

He decided there was only one person who could tell him that.

***

"Why?" Clint asked.

"I'm sorry."

Olivia had just opened the door to her room, and before entering, Clint asked the question.

"I said 'why?'"

"Why what?"

He stepped into the room and allowed her to close the door before speaking again.

"Why would someone steal your father's watch?"

"I don't know," she said.

"If you don't know," Clint said, "then I can't help you."

"What—"

"The same judge who sentenced your father to hang has made me a special investigator," Clint said. "My job is to find that watch."

"Then he's admitting it was stolen?"

"Just about," Clint said. "But before I can try to find it, I need to know why someone would steal it. And why would this sheriff and this judge, and probably the undertaker, all be hiding that fact."

Olivia sat down on the edge of the bed, her hands folded in her lap. She was wearing another very simple dress, this one emerald green.

"There's something you're not telling me," he said.

***

After Sheriff Osborne left the Judge's chamber, Samuel entered and waited.

"You got those names for me, Samuel?"

"Yes, sir."

Samuel stepped forward and laid a piece of paper down on the judge's desk.

"Very good," Judge Anderson said. "That's all."

"Yes, sir."

Samuel turned and left.

Judge Osborne picked up the slip of paper and studied the three names.

Chapter Fifteen

Sheriff Osborne entered the undertaker's establishment. Abner Weatherly looked at him right away and frowned.

"What's goin' on?" he asked.

"The Judge wants to make sure we know what we're gettin' into," Osborne said. "That we know what's at stake here."

"I don't need to know that as much as you and him," Abner said.

"How do you figure?"

"When I got him," the undertaker said, "he was already dead. The Judge sentenced 'im, and you hanged 'im."

"So you don't think you're in as deep as we are?" Osborne asked.

"I'm in it up to my neck, Sheriff," Abner said. "You tell Judge Anderson that I know that."

"Adams is probably gonna come back to you," Osborne said.

"Let 'im come."

"You need to know one thing," Osborne said, and told him what the judge had done.

"So Adams is a lawman now?" Abner asked. "That's crazy!"

"He's not a lawman," Osborne said. "I am. Adams is just a special investigator."

"That doesn't make sense."

"The Judge wants to keep an eye on Adams, know everythin' he's doin'," Osborne said. "This is the way to do it."

"Don't forget," Abner said, "this is the Gunsmith we're talkin' about."

"So do you have a better idea?" Osborne asked.

"Yes," Abner said. "I have an extra box in the back."

"You're sayin' kill Adams?"

"Shoot 'im in the back," Abner said, "and dump him in the box. I bury him. Problem solved."

Osborne stared at Abner.

"What?" the man said.

"I'm surprised, is all," Osborne said.

"By what?"

"That you're ready to kill Adams."

"Whoa, whoa," Abner said, "I don't kill people."

"But you said—"

"I want you should shoot 'im in the back," Abner said. "Then I'll do what I do, put him in the ground."

"So you want me to kill the Gunsmith."

"You've killed men before, haven't you?"

"Yeah," Osborne said, "but not like the Gunsmith."

"That's why I suggested shootin' him in the back," Abner said.

"Jesus," Osborne said, "if I did that without checkin' with the judge—"

"The Judge is an old man, Osborne," Abner said. "You and me have to get this done."

"And what about the Judge?"

"Well," Abner said, "I actually have two empty boxes in the back."

***

"What do you want me to tell you?" Olivia asked.

"Well, we could try the truth," Clint said.

"The truth is, somebody stole my dad's watch."

"That much I believe," Clint said, "but tell me more."

"Clint—"

"Why would somebody steal the watch?" Clint asked. "What's in it besides a picture of your mother?"

"Actually," she said, looking down at her hands, "there's no picture of my mother in it."

"Then what is in it?"

She looked up at him.

"If I tell you," she said, "then I'm really going to need your help."

"Let's start with you telling me," he said, "and then we'll go from there."

***

"What do you say?" Abner Weatherly asked Sheriff Osborne.

"Kill Adams."

"Yes."

"And cut the Judge out?"

"Yes."

"Just you and me," Osborne said.

Abner shrugged.

"If we need help, we can hire it," he said. "I just need to know if you're with me."

Osborne kept thinking about it.

"Look," Abner said, "I'm tired of this business, this town, and the Judge. Tell me you ain't?"

"Yeah," Osborne said, "I'm pretty tired of it."

"Then it's us?" Abner said. "You and me? That's it?"

"Yeah, okay," the sheriff said, "it's us."

"Good!"

"I just need to know one thing," Osborne said.

"What's that?"

"Where's the watch?"

Abner stared at him.

"Well?" Osborne said.

Abner wet his lips and said, "I thought you had it."

Chapter Sixteen

"A map."

"What?"

Olivia looked up at Clint.

"There's supposed to be a map inside the watch," she said. "I was meeting my father here so he could show it to me, and then we could follow it."

"A map to what?"

"What else?" she asked. "A treasure! At least, that's what he said when he wrote me."

"How could a map fit in a watch?"

"It's an oversized pocket watch," she said. "But I don't know if it had a paper map stuffed into the watch, or if it's somehow inscribed in the watch. I've never seen it."

"There's room in this watch for somebody to draw a map on it? Or, scratch it into the surface?"

She shrugged.

"The back, or the inside," she said. "Could be. I don't know. Like I said, I never saw it."

"And now it's missing," Clint said.

"Yes."

"Which means somebody killed him for it, believing there was a map inside, leading to some kind of treasure."

"I suppose so."

"How would somebody know?" Clint asked.

She made a face.

"Momma always said Poppa had a big mouth. I guess she was right."

"So who in town would he have told?" Clint asked. "Did he ever mention any partners to you? Or friends?"

"No," she said, "he never wrote that he had any friends or partners."

"What about a woman?"

"My father was sixty-six years old, Clint," she said. "I don't believe he was interested in any women."

"He was sixty-six," Clint said, "but not . . ." He stopped.

"Not dead," she said. "Was that what you were going to say?"

"Yes."

"Well, my father wasn't a good looking man, either, Clint," she said. "I don't think a woman would be interested in him, either."

"Okay, then," Clint said. "You may not know of any, but I'll have to check and see if he did have any partners, or friends."

"How do you expect to do that?"

"I can start by looking in his room," Clint said. "Or have they rented it out, already?"

"I don't know," she said. "It was just down the hall. But what good is going through his room? I have all his belongings here in a box, except the watch."

"What if the watch wasn't stolen, Olivia?" Clint asked.

"Then where is it?"

"He may have hidden it."

She squared her shoulders, as if coming to attention, and got to her feet.

"I never thought of that."

"Well," he said, "let's have a look."

***

Clint went downstairs, found out from the clerk that the room was still registered to Olivia's father.

"Nobody ever told me he checked out," the clerk said.

"I think being hanged by the neck until dead is a form of checking out," Clint said. "Don't you?"

"Uh, yessir," the young clerk said, swallowing hard.

"Let me have a key," Clint said.

"Uh, I don't know about that, sir—"

"The man's dead," Clint said. "I've been tasked by Judge Anderson to find out what happened."

"I, uh, thought he was hung."

"There are still things I have to investigate," Clint said.

"Now let me have the key to his room."

"Yessir."

The young clerk, still visibly confused, handed the key over.

Clint went upstairs, knocked on Olivia's door and said, "I have the key," when she opened it. "Do you want to come with me?"

"Yes, I do," she said.

She followed him down the hall, waited while he unlocked the door, and then they both went in.

"It looks empty," she said.

"It is empty, but let's see if there are any likely hiding places for something as small as a watch."

They started to look around the room, in the dresser and bedside table drawers, under the mattress, under the bed, and in the closet.

While they searched, Clint asked, "Olivia, do you have any idea what this treasure is?"

"No," she said, "my father only wrote of a map. He didn't say what it would lead to."

They continued the search, and then Clint stood in the center of the room.

"Nothing," he said, disappointed.

"Did you really expect to find anything?" she asked.

"No," he said, "but I was hoping."

"So what now?"

"I'm going to talk to the clerk again," Clint said. "Maybe he saw somebody coming or going with your father while he was here."

"Shall I come with you?"

"No," Clint said, "because after that I'm going to leave the hotel and start asking questions."

"Asking who?"

"I'll start with the undertaker, again," Clint said, "only this time, I have some official standing."

"Then I'll definitely stay here," she said. "I don't want to see that horrible man, again."

Clint took one more look around the room, hoping something would leap out at him, but it was to no avail.

"Okay," Clint said, "back to your room, then. We'll talk later."

Chapter Seventeen

"You're askin' if I ever saw the man they hanged with anyone else from town?" the clerk asked.

"That's what I'm asking," Clint said.

"Well," the clerk said, "I wasn't on duty the whole time he was here."

"And how long was that?"

"I'd, uh, have to look at the register."

"Then look!"

"Yessir."

The clerk brought a book out from beneath the desk and set it on top, then leafed through it.

"He was here about a week," he said.

"Let me see."

The clerk turned the book so Clint could read it. According to the date he checked in, it had now been ten days since his arrival. For him to have contacted his daughter back East he would have to do it before coming to Winslow. The fact that he told Olivia to meet him here meant that whatever he was looking for was in the area.

"And the times that you *were* on duty," Clint asked, "you never saw him with another man?"

"No, sir," the clerk said, and as Clint started to turn away he added, "not with another man."

Clint turned back.

"You saw him with a woman?"

"Yes, sir," the clerk said, "several times."

"Doing what?"

"Talkin'," the clerk said, "eatin' . . . in the dining room . . . sometimes just . . . walkin' . . . ."

"Do you know who the woman was?"

"Well, sure," the clerk said, "everybody in town knows her."

"Okay," Clint said, "tell *me* who she is."

"Her name is Verna."

"And who is Verna?" Clint said. "Come on, don't make me drag it out of you."

"She's a whore," the clerk said.

"Victor Jackson was using a whore?" Clint asked.

"Well . . . not really," the clerk said. "I mean, she never went to his room."

"And did he go to hers?"

"I—I don't know."

"Okay," Clint said, "tell me where she is and I'll ask *her*."

"Well, the whorehouse," the clerk said. "I mean . . . it *is* hers."

"She's the Madam?" Clint asked.

"Yes, that's right," he said, "she's the Madam."

"Where is this place?"

***

Olivia had said her father was too old to do anything with a woman. Obviously, she didn't know her father very well. A sixty-six-year-old man could very well be using a whore the way she was meant to be used, but there might also have been some other reason he spent time with Verna.

He followed the clerk's directions and found the whorehouse, a two story building painted a bright yellow, hence the name—according to the clerk—The Yellow Rose. Like other whorehouses in other places, it was on an edge of the town limits, probably to keep the virtuous ladies happy.

Clint approached the door and knocked. For some reason, the door was the only thing that wasn't yellow. It was red. He wondered if there was some significance to that.

When the door opened, a man stood there, staring at him. He was tall, broad shouldered, in his thirties. Clint figured him for the bouncer.

"You're too early," the man said. "Come back later."

"I'm not here as a customer," Clint said. "I'd like to talk with Verna."

"She's asleep."

"Wake her up."

"By whose authority?" the bouncer asked. "I'll get fired."

"Show her this," Clint said, handing over the order from the judge, "and tell her I want to talk about Victor Jackson."

The big bouncer took the order and said, "Wait here."

He closed the door.

Clint waited several minutes before the door opened again.

"Follow me," the man said, handing the order back.

Clint entered and followed him to what he assumed was the viewing room, where the johns interacted with the girls and picked out the one they wanted. These rooms were usually lushly and brightly furnished, and this one was no different.

"Wait here, Adams," the bouncer said. "She's gettin' dressed."

"What's your name?"

"Bruno."

"Bouncer?"

"That's right."

"I'll bet you're good at it."

That made Bruno smile just a little, and then he said, "She'll be here shortly."

Chapter Eighteen

When Verna appeared, Clint was surprised. Madams were usually retired whores, but this one looked as if she could still be working. Tall, dark-haired, full-bodied, wearing a robe that showed no skin, but molded itself to every curve. He figured this was what passed for "dressed" in a whorehouse.

"You're the Gunsmith?"

"That's right."

"Am I supposed to be impressed that you've aligned yourself with Judge Anderson?"

"I'm not aligned with him," Clint said. "I want to nail him for what he did to Victor Jackson." He thought this might be the way to get on her good side.

"Then why are you his special investigator?"

"Because he thinks that will keep me under his thumb," Clint explained.

"And will it?"

"Hell, no," Clint said. "It's the thing that's going to help me nail him."

A girl entered the room carrying a tray with a pot of coffee and two cups.

"Join me?" Verna asked Clint.

"Sure."

They both sat on the red couch and the girl put her tray down on the table in front of it.

"Thanks, Pet," Verna said.

The girl, a cute redhead, smiled and withdrew.

"You call your girls 'pet?'" Clint asked.

"No," Verna said. "That's her name."

"Oh."

She poured him a cup and handed it to him, then poured one for herself.

"What can I do for you, Mr. Special Investigator?" she asked.

"You knew Jackson?"

"So?"

"So were you friends?"

She sipped her coffee, then said, "Sort of."

"Were you . . . servicing him?"

She snorted and said, "No."

"Then—"

"Let's just leave it at us bein' friends," she said.

"Did he have any other friends in town?" Clint asked.

"No."

"Do you know anything about his watch?"

She frowned.

"His watch?"

"Yes," Clint said, "his daughter says his pocket watch is missing."

"Olivia?"

"Yes," Clint said, "didn't you know she was in town?"

"I knew he wrote to her," she said. "I—I didn't go to the hanging, and Victor told me not to come to the jail. If Olivia's here, I haven't seen her. And I doubt she wants to see an old whore who was a friend of her father's."

"Not so old," Clint said.

She smiled.

"I'm older than I look."

"So . . . do you know anything about his watch?"

"Sorry." She shook her head. "What do you think happened to it?"

"At first we thought it was stolen," Clint said, "maybe by the undertaker. But now I'm thinking maybe he hid it."

She leaned forward and put her cup down.

"Well, I don't know what happened to it," she said. "I have nothing of his, nothing to remember him by."

"Maybe," Clint said, "you should meet Olivia. She'd like to know a friend of her father's."

"You think so?"

"I know so."

"Well," Verna said, "if she wants to meet me, you know where to find me."

"I do."

She stood up.

"I have to get ready for the day's work," she said. "If you'd like to stay, I can have several of the girls come down early so you can choose one."

"That's okay," he said, standing. "I don't make a habit of visiting whorehouses for the purpose of using them."

"No," she said, "I don't suppose you have to."

She walked him to the front door.

"If anything occurs to you that you think might be . . . helpful to me," Clint said, "I hope you'll let me know. I'm at the Wicker."

"I'll let you know if I do," she promised.

She opened the door for him, stood in the doorway as he went down the steps and turned.

"If you change your mind about whores," she said, "I have some good ones."

"I bet you do," he said. "Tell me, what was it that made you become Victor Jackson's only friend in town?"

"He said he was going to come into a great deal of money," she said, "and he wanted to invest in a business."

"A whorehouse?"

She raised her eyebrows.

"Can you think of a more safe investment?" she asked.

He had a few thoughts, but he kept them to himself.

Chapter Nineteen

Clint went from the whorehouse directly to the under-taker's place. Abner Weatherly was not happy to see him.

"What do you want?" he asked.

"Just to talk."

"I don't have to talk to you."

"This says you do."

Clint handed the undertaker Judge Anderson's written order.

"Special Investigator," he said, handing it back. "How did you manage that?"

"It wasn't my idea," Clint said, pocketing the order. "It was the judge's."

"All right," Weatherly said, "what do you want?"

"I want Jackson's watch."

"Again, about the watch?" the undertaker said. "I don't know anything about it."

"Yeah, I think you do," Clint said. "I know the watch is supposed to lead the way to something worth a lot of money. I just don't know what it is. But I think you do."

"I don't have any idea what you're talkin' about," Weatherly said. "And I have work to do."

"I'm going to take a look around," Clint said.

"You mean you're going to search my place?"

"Exactly," Clint said.

"Go ahead, then," Weatherly said. "Just don't disturb my dead."

"I'll do my best not to wake them," Clint said.

***

"Wait a minute," Olivia said, staring at Clint across the table in his hotel dining room. "My father's only friend in town was a whore?"

"That's how it seems."

"And he was going to invest in her business?" Olivia asked. "A whorehouse?"

"That's what Verna said."

"And you really believe she and my father were friends?" she asked.

"They were seen together," Clint said.

"Did she watch him hang?"

"No."

"Did she testify on his behalf?"

"She didn't go to the trial," Clint said.

"Why not?"

"She says your father told her to stay away."

She made a face.

"I can't believe my father was lying with a whore."

"She says they were friends," Clint reminded her. "He wasn't a customer."

"And you believe her?"

"Actually, I do."

Olivia grew quiet and Clint took the opportunity to order for both of them.

"So what do we do now?" she asked.

"I went to the undertaker's and searched the place," Clint told her.

"Needless to say, no watch, right?" she asked.

"Right."

"Well, somebody's got it."

"I agree with you," Clint said. "Somebody's got it, but did they steal it, or did your father give it to them for safekeeping?"

"Who would he give it to?" she asked.

"A friend," Clint said.

"And you said this whore was his only friend," Olivia came back. "So you're saying she has it?"

"She said she doesn't," Clint said, "but I'm thinking she lied."

"How are you going to prove it?"

"I don't know yet."

She frowned at him.

"Are you going to sleep with her?" she demanded. "To win her over?"

"No," he said.

"Because you could," she went on.

"What?"

"You're just amazing in bed, Clint Adams," she said. "And even though she's a professional whore, I think you would win her over."

"Are you serious?"

"I'm very serious," she said.

"And you wouldn't mind?"

"Why? Because we slept together once?" she asked. "We're not a couple, Clint. I want you to do what's necessary to find that watch, and I don't care what it is."

He stared across the table at her. The waiter chose that moment to arrive with their plates.

"Don't tell me you're disappointed in me," Olivia said. "I want my father's watch."

"Eat your food," Clint said. "We'll talk about it later."

Chapter Twenty

"You're quiet," Olivia said, as they walked back through the lobby.

"I'm thinking."

"About what I said?" she asked. "About the whore? Listen, I was serious—"

"I know you were," Clint said. "That's what I'm thinking about. You actually want me to sleep with a woman to gain her trust? You know what that would make me?"

"Clint—"

"I'd be the whore," he said, not letting her break in.

They remained silent as he walked her to her room and stopped at the door.

"Do you want to come in?" she asked.

"No," he said. "I've got to figure out my next step."

"Are you mad at me?"

"Olivia," he said, "I'm not mad, I just think there's still something you're not telling me."

"Like what?"

"Let's both think about it overnight," he said, "and talk in the morning. Maybe then we'll figure it out."

He headed down the hall to his own room and didn't watch her go into hers . . .

***

. . . and he didn't have breakfast with her the next day. He left the hotel to have breakfast someplace else where he wouldn't run into her. He just wasn't ready to talk to her yet.

Her attitude about Verna had changed too drastically to suit him. First, she was shocked that her father might've slept with the whorehouse Madam, and then she turned around and told Clint he *should* sleep with her. He was starting to wonder what Olivia was more concerned with, her father or his watch?

He found a small café he had never seen before and went in. It was off the main street, and half empty. He was able to get himself a back table and ordered ham-and-eggs from the fat waiter.

While he ate, he decided he would stay involved with Olivia, but not because he wanted to help her. He wanted to satisfy his own curiosity about what "treasure" this missing watch was supposed to lead to. So he was no longer locked into a "lady in distress" situation, the kind that he usually got himself into. This was now for his own benefit.

He wasn't stuck in Winslow, he wanted to be there.

***

He left the café and went to the sheriff's office. It was his experience that most town sheriffs were crooked. It was just a matter of degrees. Some took small bribes but did their jobs, others took large bribes not to do their jobs. They were usually under somebody's thumb, like a rich rancher, a mayor . . . or a judge. Others, like the Earps, used their badges to get what they wanted, but did the job and weren't under anybody's thumb.

Still, some of them not only wore the badge for what it could get them, but because they liked it. He had to figure out which of these Sheriff Osborne was. He was under the Judge's thumb, or out to get what he could for himself?

He entered the sheriff's office and found it empty. He took the opportunity to look through the desk, although he certainly didn't think the man was dumb enough to hide the watch in a drawer. He found an extra gun, a bottle of whiskey and some old wanted posters. By the time the door opened and Osborne walked in, he had finished and was standing in front of the sheriff's desk.

"Find anything?" the sheriff asked.

"No," Clint said, "I just got here before you did."

"What's on your mind?" the sheriff said, sitting at his desk, taking his hat off and dropping it on his desk. "The Judge says I gotta help ya."

"Do you do everything the Judge tells you to do?" Clint asked.

"Not everythin'."

"So you're saying you've got a mind of your own?" Clint asked.

"What's this about?" Osborne asked.

"Just wondering."

"About what?"

"You," Clint said. "That badge, and what it means."

Osborne looked down at the tin of his chest.

"It means I'm the law."

"And what's that mean to you, Sheriff?" Clint asked.

"Do you have a point, Adams?"

"I'm just wondering if that badge means anything to you, or if you're just using it for your own benefit. Or the Judge's."

Osborne studied Clint for a few moments, then said, "I know you're the goddamned Gunsmith, Adams, and you could gun me down in a second, but get outta my office."

Clint turned, walked to the door, and said, "Just thought I'd ask," before walking out.

Chapter Twenty-One

"I want to take you to supper," Clint said.

"What?" Verna asked. "Why?"

They were standing in the doorway of her whore-house. Bruno had answered the door and told Clint that Verna was busy. Clint told him he only needed a few minutes of her time. Bruno went inside, and then Verna came out.

"Because I need to talk to someone who knows everyone in town."

"I don't know everyone," she said.

"You know the men," he said. "That'll be good enough."

She studied him for a moment.

"Are you going to take me somewhere nice?"

"You name it," Clint said. "Anyplace you want."

"Pick me up at six," she said, and went back inside.

Clint walked away. He didn't get far when he felt someone coming up behind him, so he turned quickly and found himself facing Bruno.

"Don't do anythin' that'll hurt Verna," the bouncer said. "If you do, you'll have to deal with me, and I don't care who you are."

"I'm not looking to hurt her," Clint said. "I just need her knowledge."

"The so called good people of this town look down at her," Bruno said.

"The good women of this town, you mean."

"Yes."

"What makes you think I'd hurt her?"

"She's gonna have you take her to the best restaurant in town," Bruno said. "That's where all those good people will be."

"I see," Clint said. "You think I should take her somewhere else?"

"She won't let you do that," Bruno said. "When Verna makes up her mind, that's it. I just want you to protect her."

"Like you do."

"That's right."

"Don't worry," he said. "I won't let anybody hurt her."

Bruno nodded, turned and went back to the house.

***

Clint returned to the whorehouse at six o'clock, found Verna waiting for him, wearing a dress that covered her from neck to ankles in vivid blue.

"Ready?" she asked.

"I don't know," he said. "Should I have dressed better?"

"Don't worry," she said. "The place I'm having you take me, would hate having us there no matter how you were dressed."

"Oh."

"Shall we go?"

"Can we walk?"

"Yes," she said. "It's not far."

As they left her office and headed for the door, a tall blonde approached, looking agitated.

"Verna, those Bailey brothers are here again—"

Verna held her hand up to stop the woman.

"Take it up with Samantha, she's in charge tonight," she said. "And talk to Bruno. If they need taking care of, he'll do it. I'm going to supper."

"Out?" the woman asked. "You're goin' out?"

"That's right."

The woman looked at Clint, then back at Verna. Finally, she smiled.

"Have a good time," she said.

"I plan to," Verna said. She looked at Clint and asked again, "Shall we go?"

Chapter Twenty-Two

"There it is," Verna said, when they were still several hundred feet away. "The best restaurant in Winslow."

"What's it called?" Clint asked. "Seems to me folks hereabouts name their businesses after themselves."

"That's right," she said. "You're in the Wicker Hotel. No, this is called The Winslow House."

"Really?" he asked. "That shows even less imagination than using your own name."

"That might be," she said, "but they do serve the best food in Winslow. Or so I've been told."

"You've never been there?" he asked.

"No."

"Well, let's go, then."

They covered the last hundred feet and entered the restaurant. A man wearing a dark suit confronted them at the door.

"Do you have a reservation?" he asked.

"What?" Clint asked. "No, we don't." He had only heard of restaurants in major cities, like New York, Denver and San Francisco, taking reservations.

"Then I'm sorry—"

"Take a look at this," Clint said, handing him the order from the Judge.

The man unfolded the paper and read it. He was in his fifties, and Clint had the feeling the Judge's signature at the bottom was going to mean something to him.

"Signed by Judge Anderson," he said, impressed.

"That's right."

The man turned and looked at the other diners, who were looking up from their tables at the new entrants.

"That's right."

The man handed Clint back the order, then looked at Verna, who smiled at him.

"A table for two?" the man asked.

"Yes," Clint said, "in the back, against the wall."

It was men like Clint and Wyatt Earp and Bat Masterson who wanted tables like that, and since there weren't any of those types in town, all the tables against the back wall were empty.

"Yes, of course, this way."

He led them across the floor to the back, with Verna drawing withering looks from the "good" ladies who were seated with their husbands.

"Your waiter will be with you in a minute," the man said.

"Thank you," Verna said. As he walked away, she said to Clint, "That was very satisfying."

"Yes, I noticed you got lots of attention."

"They're still looking over here with their prune faces," Verna said.

"I assume you saw some customers of yours as we walked back here."

"Oh yes," she said. "They're the men making sure they don't look over here."

A young waiter came over and Clint said to Verna, "Well, you're the one who's heard about this place, so why don't you order for both of us."

"All right."

She ordered steak for Clint, and venison for herself, and then a bottle of wine.

"We can taste each other's," she said, as the waiter went to the kitchen. He came back quickly with the bottle of red wine, and poured for each of them. Clint wasn't really a wine lover, but he had left it up to Verna to order, so he lifted his glass and toasted with her.

"Here's to a fine meal," she said, and they clinked glasses. "Now, what was it you wanted to talk about?"

"I need information on three men," he said. "Judge Anderson, Abner Weatherly, and Sheriff Osborne."

"You might find this hard to believe," she said, "but none of those three have ever been to my house."

"Really?" he asked. "I suppose I could believe that of the judge, but the other two?"

"Well," she said. "Osborne wears a badge, and he needs votes to keep wearing it. The good women of this town don't vote, but they control their husbands."

"And Weatherly?"

"I don't think he likes women."

"You mean—"

"No," she said, "I mean, I don't think he has any interest in sex."

"So then you're telling me you don't know anything about them?"

"Oh, I wouldn't want you to think you're wasting this meal," she said. "I think I can come up with something to tell you about each of them."

"That's good," he said. "I'm all ears."

***

Verna talked the entire time they were eating. Most of what she had to say about the judge, the undertaker and the sheriff were things she had heard from her customers.

This was what Clint came away with:

The Judge was old, ornery, cantankerous, and arrogant; The Undertaker was a thief, like his father, but he was the only undertaker in town, so folks who had their loved ones buried expected a few "little things" to go missing; The Sheriff was lazy and pretty much did what the judge told him to do, but the town had worse sheriffs before him.

"Is he crooked?" Clint asked.

"What's crooked mean?" Verna asked. "He's not a thief, like Abner Weatherly, but he's been known to take a bribe or two. Is that crooked?"

"That's about normal for the job," Clint observed.

"Were you ever a lawman?"

"Years ago," Clint said, "when I was young."

"And were you crooked?"

Clint hesitated then said, "I took a free meal or drink when it was offered."

"So there you go," she said. "Certain things come with the job."

After they finished their meals, Verna ordered dessert for both of them.

"Anything but rhubarb," Clint said, so she asked for two slices of apple pie. Clint's favorite was peach, but he took the apple.

***

"How was everything?" he asked, as they walked back to her house later.

"The food was okay," she said. "I've had better at a couple of small cafes in town. But the looks we were gettin' was the best part." She laughed. "I've gotta thank you for that."

"Has anything else occurred to you?" he asked.

"About what?"

"About Jackson, and his watch."

"Oh, that," she said. "No, nothin'."

They stopped in front of her house.

"You wanna come in?" she asked. "I'll have one of the girls give you a free poke."

"That's okay," he said. "Thanks for all the infor-mation."

"You don't much like whores, do you?" she asked.

"I've known lots of whores I liked a lot," he said. "I just don't use them. In fact, I like you."

The last comment seemed to bother her. She frowned, was almost on the verge of saying something, but instead said, "Thanks for supper."

Before Clint could even say she was welcome, she went inside, the door slamming behind her.

Chapter Twenty-Three

Clint walked to Bill Jellicoe's Saloon, found it doing a pretty good business. The gaming tables were going, as was the piano. The bar was busy, and most of the tables were taken. There were three girls working the floor. He went to the bar and managed to elbow himself a space.

Jelly spotted him and came right over.

"What can I getcha?"

"Beer."

"Comin' up."

As Jelly went to get the beer, a man came over to Clint and said, "Hey, you were in the Winslow House tonight with Verna."

"That's right," Clint said. "I was."

The man, a large fellow in his forties, said, "Well, let me shake your hand."

Clint shook the man's hand briskly, then reclaimed his so it would be free to grab his gun if he had to.

"What am I being congratulated for?" he asked.

"I was havin' supper at the Winslow with my wife when you came in, and after that she couldn't swallow a thing," the man said, with a big grin. "And a lot of the other women in there had the same problem."

"I assume you've been a customer of Verna's?"

"Her whorehouse, yeah," the man said. "Not her. I go there to see a gal named Penny. See, my wife's gotten big as a house, and she don't like doin' nothin' in bed any-more." He laughed. "Maybe after tonight she'll lose some weight. Anyway, I just wanted to say thanks. It was funny as hell."

He turned and went back to a table where he'd been sitting with a couple of friends.

Clint turned back to the bar.

"Who was that?" he asked Jelly.

"His name's Zack Farrell," Jelly said. "Owns the hardware store."

"Hey," Clint said, "does this town have a town coun-cil? A mayor?"

"We sure do," Jelly said, "and they're good for nothin'."

"Why's that?"

"Because they go along with Judge Anderson on eve-ry decision," Jelly said.

"I thought the mayor was supposed to run a town."

"Not this one," Jelly said. "He's just a—whatayacallit—somethin' with the head?"

"A figurehead?"

"That's it!" Jelly said, pointing. "A figurehead."

"Why does everybody go along with Judge Ander-son?" Clint asked.

"You know," Jelly said, "I ain't sure about that. Maybe while you're here you can find out."

Jelly went to serve some other customers then and Clint stood there with his beer, thinking maybe he was going to have to do just that.

Chapter Twenty-Four

"You're back."

He turned from the bar, saw the brunette, Annie, standing there.

"I'm back," he said.

"Lookin' for me?" she asked.

"Why not?" he asked.

"I just thought you might wanna talk to somebody who knows things," she said.

"And that's you?"

"Oh yeah," she said. "People in a saloon talk all the time, and I listen."

"So what do you know?"

"Not here," she said. "I have a room upstairs."

"Let's go."

"Not now," she said. "I'm too busy. Come back in three hours, when I get off."

"Maybe I'll just hang around until then," he said. "I've got nothing else to do."

"Do some gambling, then," she said, "I'll find you."

He raised his mug to her, and she melted back into the crowd.

Clint finished his beer, then went to find a poker game . . .

***

He felt a hand on his shoulder as he was raking in another pot. Then he felt her breath on his ear.

"I'm ready if you are."

"That's it for me boys," he said, pushing his chair back and picking up his money. "Maybe tomorrow night."

"You can't leave now," the man seated across from him said, "you're ahead."

"Is that your rule?" Clint asked. "What makes you such a good gambler? Never leave the table while you're ahead?"

"No," the man said, "that's my rule for you. You don't leave the table with my money."

His name was Wes Cantrell, and he was winning until Clint sat down. Now he'd been losing for two hours and wasn't happy about it. He was wearing a gambler's black suit, and Clint saw the gun bulge under his arm when he first sat down. He'd been in a real good mood at that time, but now he was in a foul one.

"Honey, come back later for your friend. He's still got some work to do, here."

"My name's Annie," she said. "Don't call me honey."

"How about bitch?" Cantrell asked. "Can I call you bitch?"

"Hey," Clint said, "take it easy. That's no way to talk to a lady."

"She's a saloon girl," Cantrell said. "Not a lady."

"Hey!" Annie screamed.

"Shut up!" Cantrell said. "You, siddown. And you," he pointed to another man at the table, "deal."

Clint pointed at the same man and said, "Deal me out."

"Did you hear what I said?" Cantrell asked. He started to slide his chair back.

"If you stand up," Clint said, "this is going to get ugly."

The other three players at the table—all local shop owners—pushed their chairs back. Customers around the table sensed what was happening and spread out.

"You really want to go there?" the gambler asked.

"No," Clint said, "but you do, apparently."

"Maybe you didn't get my name," the gambler said. "It's Cantrell, Wes Cantrell."

"Is that supposed to mean something to me?" Clint asked.

"No, but maybe my brother's name means somethin' to you," Cantrell said. "Red Cantrell."

Clint stared at Cantrell for a minute.

"Well, yeah," he said, "I know that name."

"So then you'll sit back down and play," Cantrell said, as if it was a done deal.

"No, I won't."

"You know who Red Cantrell is, right?" Cantrell asked. "The fastest gun in the West? Killed a dozen men?"

"I know he's said to be the current fastest gun," Clint said, "and he's supposedly killed a dozen men."

"You sayin' my brother's rep ain't true?"

"I'm sayin' no man's rep is true," Clint said. "Your brother's, mine—"

"You have a reputation?" Cantrell asked, with a doubtful look.

"Don't make me prove it, Cantrell," Clint said. "Go back to your game and maybe I'll see you tomorrow."

Clint started to turn, but Cantrell jumped to his feet.

"You're not leavin' with my money!" he said. His hand darted into his coat for the gun that was under his left arm.

Clint drew and fired. He had no way of knowing how good Cantrell was, especially since his brother was a proven gunman. So he had no choice. His shot hit the man in the chest, killing him instantly. He dropped to the floor.

Clint looked at Annie.

"I guess we won't be going up to your room tonight."

Chapter Twenty-Five

Sheriff Osborne came into the saloon and looked down at the dead man.

"Wes Cantrell," he said.

"Yes," Clint said.

"Do you know who his brother is?"

"He told me."

"When Red Cantrell hears about this—"

"I know that, too."

"All right," the lawman said aloud, "a few of you men carry the body over to Abner Weatherly's. Adams, you come with me to my office."

"Lead the way," Clint said.

***

In Osborne's office he said, "Sit down."

Clint remained standing.

"Please."

Clint sat.

"I was hoping this wouldn't happen," the sheriff said, seating himself. "The Judge is gonna have a fit. He's gonna want me to run you out of town."

"Is that right?" Clint asked. "How are you going to do that, Sheriff?"

"I have eight men I can put a badge on at a moment's notice," Osborne said.

"Eight deputies," Clint said. "That's a lot."

"Will you go up against nine lawmen?" Osborne asked.

"I don't want to shoot anyone who's wearing a badge, Sheriff."

"That's good news."

"But I don't want to leave town."

"But the Judge—"

"Leave the Judge to me," Clint said.

Osborne looked skeptical.

"You're not gonna shoot the Judge, are you?"

"No."

"Okay, then. What about Red Cantrell?"

"What about him?"

"Everybody says he's it," Osborne said, "he's the fastest gun. He's gonna come here when he hears what happened."

"That's my problem, isn't it?"

"Adams," Osborne said, "it's been years since anybody said you were the fastest."

"They've said it about all of us," Clint said. "Hardin, Hickok, Ben Thompson . . . Red Cantrell is just the latest on the list. Next year it'll be somebody else."

"But we're dealin' with this year," Osborne pointed out.

"Look at it this way," Clint said, "Red Cantrell versus Clint Adams. It'll put Winslow on the map. How do you think the judge would react to that?"

The Sheriff made a face.

"He'd probably like it," he admitted.

"Like I said, I'll handle the judge."

"Well, you're probably gonna hafta do it tomorrow, when he gets this news," Osborne said. "But I gotta say, I ain't too sad about not havin' Wes Cantrell around, anymore. He was a real pain in the ass, livin' off his brother's rep."

"I'm sorry it happened the way it did," Clint said. "I tried to avoid it. There was no reason for it except his stupidity."

"All right," Osborne said, "get outta here. Look for the judge to send me after you tomorrow."

"I'll be ready."

Clint got up and left the sheriff's office. Outside he found the saloon girl, Annie, waiting for him. She had a shawl on to cover her bare shoulders.

"What are you doing here?" he asked.

"I thought maybe you'd want some company," she said. "Maybe we could revisit the idea of goin' up to my room. I still got things I could tell you."

"Sure, why not?" he asked. "I'm not in the mood to go to my hotel and sit alone in my room."

"I could go there with you," she offered.

"No," he said, "I'd rather be somewhere tonight that nobody knows about. Cantrell might have some friends."

"I don't think he had many friends in town," she said, "but we can go out the back way and nobody'll see us."

"I'm in your hands, then," he said, and she led the way.

***

They entered the saloon through a back door and went up a dark stairway. It occurred to him that she might be leading him into some kind of trap, but it turned out not to be the case.

She unlocked the door to her room while he listened to some of the noise from downstairs.

"The saloon is still open?" he asked.

"Yeah," she said, "but I'm done for the night."

She led him into the room, and locked the door behind them, then removed her shawl. There was already a lamp lit on the table next to the bed, so she walked to it and turned it up. It bathed her lovely skin in a yellow light.

She approached him and reached for his belt.

"Annie—"

She smiled at him.

"You said you were in my hands," she reminded him.

"I did say that, didn't I?"

Chapter Twenty-Six

She got him naked and actually did take him into her hands. She stroked his hard cock until it was harder, then undressed herself quickly. She was a slender girl with small, pretty breasts, slim hips and a bushy patch between her legs that immediately drew his eyes. She couldn't keep her hands off his penis.

They tumbled onto the bed together, each trying to get to the other's crotch. She alternately gripped his cock tightly, and stroked it, while he reached down to probe through the bush to find her slick and wet.

***

Sheriff Osborne knocked on the door of Judge Anderson's house. The Judge answered it himself, holding a drink in his hand.

"Come in, Sheriff," he said. He turned and walked away, leaving Osborne to close the door and follow him.

When the sheriff got to the living room, the judge was seated in a large, comfortable chair.

"Drink?" the Judge offered.

"No, sir, thanks."

"What's on your mind?"

"Wes Cantrell."

"That buffoon?" the Judge snapped. "What about him?"

"He's dead."

"How?"

"Shot."

"Where?"

"The saloon, at a card game."

"That figures," the Judge said. "Who killed him?"

"The Gunsmith."

Anderson stopped with his glass halfway to his mouth.

"Oh."

"This is gonna bring Red Cantrell to town," Osborne said, "probably within a day or two."

"Do we know where he is?"

"No, but he'll make it," Osborne said. "Do you want me to get Adams out of town?"

"Why would I want you to do that?" the Judge asked. "This could solve our problem."

"You think Red Cantrell can take Clint Adams?"

"I think we're going to find out," the Judge said. "And whatever happens will be good for Winslow."

"So I'm supposed to just let it happen?"

"Stick a badge on a few deputies," Anderson said. "If Cantrell kills Adams, I want him out of town."

"And if Adams kills Cantrell?"

"Then we're no worse off than we are now."

"I suppose—"

"Did you take Adams in after the shooting?" Anderson asked.

"Yes," Osborne said. "We talked in my office, but there were witnesses that Wes Cantrell pushed it, and went for his gun first."

"I believe it."

"I think Adams might be comin' to see you tomorrow, Judge," Osborne said.

"About this?"

"Yeah."

"Let him," the Judge said. "I'd like to hear what he has to say. Also, I'll get a progress report on his investigation."

"All right."

Osborne turned to leave.

"Where are we on the watch, Sheriff?"

The lawman turned back.

"I, uh, thought Abner had it."

"And he doesn't?"

"He says he thought I had it."

"And do you?"

"Uh, no."

The judge looked into his glass, then back at Sheriff Osborne.

"This is . . . disconcerting," he said, finally.

"Sir?"

"I'm annoyed, Sheriff!" the Judge snapped. "Adams is looking for that watch, and now we are, when I thought we already had it."

"Yes sir."

The Judge pinned Osborne with a hard stare. He looked for all the world liked a wizened old man—except for when he stared at someone that way.

"Find that watch, Sheriff," the Judge said. "Your . . . job depends on it."

"I'll find it, Judge."

"And don't let Abner pull the wool over your eyes," Anderson said. "His father was good at that. But he's not as good at it."

"I'll keep that in mind."

The Judge sipped from his glass.

"See yourself to the door," he said, "and make sure you pull it shut on your way out."

Chapter Twenty-Seven

They wrestled around on the bed for a short time, each trying for the advantage. Finally, Clint's superior size worked to his advantage, and he pinned her down on her back. He slithered down between her legs, held her thighs down with his elbows, and pressed his face to that dark patch of hair. First he inhaled her fragrance, then poked through with his tongue, tasting her. She gasped as the tip of his tongue came into contact with her vagina, then reached down to hold his head there. He continued his oral exploration, enjoying the nectar that gushed from her as a result of it. Then mounting her, he plunged his hard cock into her. She gasped, her eyes widened, and then she smiled. It was a dreamy smile that stayed on her face until she bit her lips to keep from screaming . . .

***

"You said you had some things you could tell me," he reminded her, later.

They were lying side-by-side on their backs.

"I do," Annie said, "I just thought we'd spend some time gettin' better acquainted, first."

"Well," he said, "I think we've done that, don't you?"

"Oh, yes . . ."

"Then what've you got for me?"

"Well . . . I was going to warn you about Wes Cantrell when you sat down at that poker table."

"No need for that, now," he said. "What else?"

"Well . . . who do you want to know about?" she rolled over onto her side to look at him. "It might be easier to do it that way."

"Tell me about the sheriff."

"He got elected because he was backed by Judge Anderson," she said. "He pretty much does what the Judge wants him to do."

"Why not vote him out?" Clint asked.

"Like I said, he's backed by the Judge," she said. "Nobody will run against him."

"So he's got a job for life?"

"Or," she said, "for the life of the Judge."

"Okay," he said, "Tell me about Abner Weatherly."

"A thief, like his father before him," she said. "He's got no friends, never comes into the Saloon, but everybody has to go to him when someone dies because he's the only undertaker we have."

So far she had told him things he already knew.

"Okay," he said, "now tell me about Verna, the madam at the whorehouse."

Annie's smile broadened.

"Oh, Verna. I like 'er."

"How well do you know her?"

"Very well," she said.

"Have you worked for her?"

"No," she said, "I'm a saloon girl, not a whore. She's offered me a job several times, but understands when I tell her no."

"So then how do you know her?"

"She was friends with my mother," she said. "And when my mother died, Verna took me under her wing."

"How long ago was that?"

"Ten years or so," she said. "I was fourteen when my mother died."

"So Verna became like a mother to you?"

"More like an older sister," Annie said.

"Did you know Victor Jackson?"

"Just to see him in the saloon," she said. "He was only here a couple of weeks, but he seemed to become friends with Verna."

"Friends?" Clint asked. "Not a customer?"

"Not of Verna's," Annie said. "She doesn't see men, anymore."

"So he could have been seeing one of her girls?"

"It's possible," she said, "but he was kind of old. I thought they were just friends."

"Do you know the girls who work for Verna?"

"Most of them," she said. "Some are from here. The ones she hired from out of town, not as well."

"Could you find out for me if Jackson was using any of them?"

"Sure," she said, "I could ask."

"Okay," he said.

"Anythin' else?" she asked.

"Do you know Red Cantrell?"

"Never seen 'im," she said. "Only heard about him from his brother, who was always tellin' people he was Red's brother."

"Is there anyone else in town you might want to warn me about?"

She considered that for a moment, then said, "Not that I can think of right now." She ran her hand down over his belly, down further until she had his semi-hard cock in her hand, again. "Except maybe me?"

Before he could say anything, she slid down between his legs and took him into her hot mouth . . .

Chapter Twenty-Eight

Clint decided not to spend the night in Annie's room, so he left the building the same way they had come in, by the back door. He walked back to the Wicker Hotel and entered the lobby. As he did, he saw Sheriff Osborne sitting on a sofa against the wall. When the lawman saw him, he stood up.

"I've been waitin' for you," Osborne said.

"Have you decided to arrest me?" Clint asked. "Or run me out of town?"

"Neither," the lawman said. "The Judge said he'll see you tomorrow, if you like."

"Ah, you told him what happened."

"Yeah."

"Was he upset?"

"Not at all," Osborne said. "He thinks whether you kill Red Cantrell, or he kills you, Winslow benefits."

"That's what I thought he'd say," Clint reminded him.

"Uh, yeah, right," Osborne said.

"Anything else? Clint asked. "I was on my way to turn in for the night."

"No," Osborne said, "I just thought I'd warn you."

He started for the door.

"Sheriff?" Clint called.

The man stopped and turned.

"Why?"

"Why what?" Osborne asked.

"Why warn me?" Clint asked. "Don't you work for the Judge?"

"I suppose I do," Osborne said, "but I also work for the law." He shrugged. "I guess that's just startin' to mean somethin' to me."

He turned and left the hotel.

Clint wondered if Sheriff Osborne was telling the truth and, if so, if he really was starting to believe he served the law, what would that mean for the search for Victor Jackson's watch?

He went to his room and turned in.

***

When Clint came down to the lobby the next morning, someone else was waiting for him. This time, it was Olivia Jackson, sitting on the same couch that Sheriff Osborne had been on the night before.

"Good-morning, Olivia."

"Clint," she said, standing up quickly. "I knocked on your door last night."

"I came in late."

"Have you found out anything?" she asked.

"Let's talk over breakfast," he suggested. "Is here in the hotel good?"

"It's fine."

They got seated, ordered breakfast and then Clint looked across the table at her.

"I haven't found out anything about the watch, but I'm trying to understand exactly what your father's relationship with Verna was."

"The hooker?"

"The madam."

"What about one of her girls?"

"I don't think your father was with any of them," Clint said, "but I'm finding out for sure."

They paused while the waiter set down their plates and poured coffee.

"Anything else?" she asked, eating a piece of bacon.

"Yes," he said, "I had to kill a man last night."

"Omigod, why?"

He explained it to her while they ate their breakfast.

"So his brother is a famous gunfighter," she said, "and he's going to come here looking for you?"

"No doubt."

"And you're going to wait for him?"

"I'm not finished looking for your father's watch," he answered.

"Forget the watch, Clint," she said. "Get out of town before he comes here."

"I can't do that," he said.

"Why not?"

"Because word would get around that I ran from a confrontation," he said. "Once that happens, I'd be finished. Men would come from all corners of the country to try me, and eventually, one of them would be faster."

"What about Red Cantrell?" she asked. "What if he turns out to be faster?"

"That day is going to come, Olivia," he said. "That's the way I'm going to die, from a bullet. I know that. It's how I live my life."

"Knowing that eventually somebody will kill you?"

"Yes."

"How can you live like that?"

"I don't have much of a choice," he said. "It's not like I can start working as a store clerk or a bank teller."

"Well," she said, "I want my father's watch, but I don't want to trade it for your life."

"Whatever happens between me and Red Cantrell, it's got nothing to do with you or the watch."

"Well," she said, "you've managed to become somebody I care about, and I don't want to lose two of you in the same damn town!"

Chapter Twenty-Nine

Now Clint had to keep looking over his shoulder for Red Cantrell while he was searching for the watch.

Olivia told him she had seen a hat shop she wanted to go to, so outside the hotel they separated.

Clint walked in an aimless manner, his eyes aware while he mulled the problem. He saw many possibilities, here. One: Jackson lost the watch. Two: he sold it. Three: he gave it to someone for safekeeping. The other possibilities were four, five and six; the undertaker had it, the sheriff had it, or the Judge had it. And then there was Verna. She was seven.

The problem was, which of these seemed the most likely?

If the watch was as important to her father as Olivia said it was, he would have taken steps to protect it. He would never have forgotten or sold it. So one and two were out.

Then there was three, he gave it to someone for safekeeping. That seemed likely, given its importance, and that would eliminate four, five and six. But three and seven would go together very nicely.

That made it likely Verna had the watch, even though she claimed not to. And if, as Olivia said, the watch lead to some sort of treasure, then Verna wasn't going to give it up.

But if she had it, and the Judge was going to have Sheriff Osborne out there looking for it, would Osborne have these same thoughts? Would he go after Verna?

Clint decided he had to get there first. His aimless stroll became a brisk walk to the whorehouse.

***

"Why are you always early?" Bruno asked him at the door.

"I just try to get here when Verna's not busy."

"But when she's asleep?"

"I think she'll see me," Clint said. "Why not ask her?"

"Wait here."

Bruno closed the door in his face and Clint wondered how involved Bruno was in Verna's business?

After a few minutes Bruno returned, opened the door and said, "This way."

Clint entered and followed him down a hallway.

"Isn't her office the other way?" he asked.

"She wants to see you in her room," Bruno said, obviously not happy about it.

When they reached the door, Bruno knocked and opened it. As Clint started past him the big man said, "Remember what I told you last time."

"How could I forget?"

He stepped in and closed the door in Bruno's face.

Verna was seated at a dressing table, looking into her mirror. She was wearing a robe with a fur collar.

"Good-morning," she greeted him, looking at him in the mirror.

"I'm sorry to wake you," Clint said.

"You didn't," Verna said. "I was already sitting right here, doing my face and my hair." She turned in her chair to look directly at him. Her face and hair were expertly done, and she looked beautiful. "What can I do for you, Clint?"

"I've been thinking," he said, "and I believe Victor gave you his watch." He had decided to take the direct approach.

"Why would he do that?"

"For safekeeping."

"And what was so important about this watch?"

"I've been told it can lead to some kind of treasure," Clint said. "I don't know what he told you. Maybe he just said it was an heirloom and he wanted to save it for Olivia."

"No," she said, "you were right the first time."

"About the treasure?"

"About him giving it to me to safeguard," she said. "But he never said it was an heirloom."

"What did he say it was?"

"Something very important," she said.

"That was it?"

She spread her hands.

"That's it."

"And where is it?"

"I don't have it."

"Why not?"

She looked embarrassed.

"It was stolen."

"Verna—"

"I know," she said. "You thought you'd figured it out, and you're right, but . . . I don't have it, anymore."

"When was it stolen?"

"The day they hanged him I went looking, and it wasn't where I had put it."

"And where was that?"

She turned and pointed at a drawer in her dressing table.

"You put it in there, for safekeeping?" he asked.

"Where did you expect?" she asked. "A bank vault? It didn't occur to me that anyone would come in here and steal it. I mean, after all, it's just a watch."

"And did you know that people were looking for it?" he asked.

"Only when you mentioned it."

"Why didn't you tell me then?"

"I didn't know you," she said.

"You don't know me much better now," he pointed out.

"Yes, but you've figured it out," she said. "And you're lookin' for it. At least this way you can take me out of the runnin'."

"All right, then," he said, "suppose you tell me who you think stole it?"

Chapter Thirty

"I don't know."

"Bruno?"

"Wha—no," she said. "He would never steal from me."

"He's in love with you."

"Um, well, yes."

"What about one of the girls?"

"Why would they?" she asked. "And how would they know about it? No, the girls never come in here."

"So you have no ideas?" he asked.

She shrugged.

"Just somebody from outside."

"And how would they get in here to steal it?" he asked.

"It's easy to get into a whorehouse, Clint," she told him. "You just come in and choose a girl."

"And whoever did it had help from the girl he chose?" he asked.

"I doubt it," she said. "They probably snuck in here."

"How easy would that've been?" Clint asked.

"That would depend on how busy we were."

"Has the sheriff been here to talk to you about it?" Clint asked.

"No," she said. "Will he?"

"I don't know if he'll figure it out."

"He's not very smart," she observed.

"We'll have to wait and see," Clint said. "I'm sure Judge Anderson has him out looking for it."

"I thought he had you out looking?"

"He thinks he has," Clint said. "That order was just his way of trying to control me."

"But he can't."

"No."

"What's this I heard about Wes Cantrell?"

"What'd you hear?"

"That you killed him."

"That's right," he said. "He didn't leave me any choice."

"Then you're gonna have to deal with Red."

"Do you know Red?"

"Just from the times he was here," she said. "He's a cruel man, damaged a couple of my girls."

"Well," Clint said, "I'll deal with him when the time comes. Right now, I want to find that watch."

"So you can find the treasure?" she asked.

"No," he said, "so I can give it to Olivia. It's rightfully hers."

"And you're not interested in what this treasure is?" she asked.

"No, I'm not."

"Then you're probably the only one."

She turned back to her mirror.

"Verna, are you sure Victor didn't mention it to you?" he asked. "Exactly what it is this watch can lead to? I mean, he trusted you enough to give you the watch for safekeeping."

"Apparently, he didn't trust me enough to tell me everythin'," she said.

"And why did he trust you, at all?"

"We were friends."

"In the short time he was here you became friends?"

She didn't answer.

"Wait a minute," Clint said. "You and he knew each other before he came here."

She turned again to look at him.

"Is that why he was here in the first place?" he asked. "To see you?"

She hesitated, then said, "Yes."

"And why did he send for Olivia?"

She looked in her mirror.

"You'll have to ask her," she said.

"Where did you know each other before?" he asked.

"Back East somewhere," she said. "It was a long time ago."

"Then why did he come here?"

"Obviously, to give me the watch," she said. "And then I lost it. So I guess he should've stayed away." She shook her head. "That's all I have to tell you. Bruno will show you out."

He started for the door, then stopped.

"Somethin' else?" she asked.

"You and Bruno," he said, "are you—"

"No," she said, cutting him off. "He's in love with me, but he works for me. That's all."

He nodded and left.

Bruno was in the hall. Clint had no way of knowing if the man had heard anything through the door.

"Finished?" he asked.

"Yes."

"Did you upset her?"

"You'll have to ask her that."

"Don't worry," the big man said. "I will."

He led Clint down to the front door, opened it and didn't say anything else. After Clint walked out, Bruno slammed it shut, forcefully.

There was something Verna wasn't telling him, but at least he'd learned a few things he didn't know before.

Chapter Thirty-One

Clint was walking back toward Olivia's hotel, wondering if she'd finished her hat shopping. On the way he saw Sheriff Osborne coming toward him.

"Adams," Osborne said, as they stopped. "I was wonderin' where you were."

"Why?"

"I was just wonderin' if you found the, uh, watch?"

"If I had," Clint said, "I wouldn't tell you, Sheriff."

"Why not?"

"Because then you'd tell the Judge."

"But if you find it," Osborne said, "ain't you gonna tell the Judge?"

"No."

"But he made you his special investigator so you'd—"

"Sheriff," Clint said, "he made me his investigator as a joke. I'm sure he's got you out looking for the watch."

"Well, yeah, but—"

"I've got to go," Clint said.

"Do you wanna see the Judge today?" the lawman asked. "I could take you over."

"No, thanks."

"Have you given any thought to what you'll do when Red Cantrell gets here?"

"What will there be for me to do except not let him kill me?" Clint asked.

Before Osborne could say anything else, Clint started walking away.

***

When Clint knocked on Olivia's door, there was no answer. Could she be trying on hats all this time? He left the hotel and went looking for the hat shop. Eventually, he found it and went inside. It had the painfully clever name above the door of HATS OFF, and a window filled with frilly hats.

"Can I help you, sir?" the middle-aged female clerk asked from behind the counter,

"I was looking for a lady who told me she was going hat shopping," he said. He described Olivia to the woman. "Was she here?"

"I haven't seen a woman like that here today, sir," the lady said.

"Is there another store in town that sells hats?"

"Not women's hats," she said, "We're the only one. The mercantile sells hats for men."

"Okay," he said, "thank you."

He left the store, stopped just outside. Olivia had either changed her mind, or lied to him.

Or she'd been taken!

***

Clint went back to Olivia's hotel and talked to the desk clerk.

"Ain't seen that lady since she left here this mornin'," the man said.

"Thanks."

He went back outside. It stood to reason that if someone had snatched the watch, they might also have snatched Olivia. Maybe they thought they needed both to find the treasure. There might have been some secret to the watch they thought she knew the answer to.

He went to the sheriff's office next.

***

Osborne was sitting behind his desk when Clint walked in.

"Adams, I didn't expect to see you—"

"I've got one question to ask you," Clint said, "and you better tell me the truth."

"What are you talkin'—"

"Did the Judge tell you to grab Olivia Jackson?" Clint asked.

"What? No! Even if he did, I wouldn't . . . are you talkin' about kidnappin'?"

"Possibly."

"Wait a minute," the lawman said. "Are you thinkin' whoever stole the watch has now grabbed her?"

"She told me she was going shopping for a hat, and she never got there," Clint said.

"She coulda changed her mind. You know how women are."

"I considered that," Clint said.

"So you don't have any proof she was taken?"

"No."

Osborne stood up.

"Where are you going?" Clint asked.

"I think we better start lookin', don't you?" the sheriff asked.

They left the office together.

"You go that way, I'll go this way," Osborne said, pointing.

"Sheriff, tell me something," Clint said. "Would the Judge have sent someone else to grab her, without telling you?"

"It's possible," Osborne said. "To tell you the truth, I been suspectin' he's lookin' to replace me. This whole watch thing might just give him the excuse to do it."

They went their separate ways.

Chapter Thirty-Two

Clint had the feeling things in Winslow were going to change. Osborne might be developing into a genuine lawman, while Judge Anderson was getting on in years and might lose his grip on the town. And they just needed a second undertaker for Abner Weatherly to lose his business so he couldn't steal from the dead, anymore.

If Olivia hadn't suddenly gone missing, he might've convinced himself to concentrate on Weatherly. Everyone seemed to know that the undertaker was a thief. On the other hand, Verna claimed he was never in her place of business.

So, undertaker aside, he had to find Olivia.

***

Sheriff Osborne entered the Judge's chamber.

"I didn't send for you," Anderson said.

"I know," Osborne said. "I just wanted to let you know Adams wouldn't be comin' in to see you today."

"Why not?"

"He doesn't feel it's necessary."

Anderson sat back in his chair.

"Has he found the watch?" he asked.

"I don't think so."

"Have you found it?"

"No."

Anderson sat forward and looked down at his desk.

"Then get out and find it."

Osborne turned and left.

***

Clint walked around town, wondering what other stores may have lured her away from her goal of a new hat. On the other hand, had she simply lied to him, and had no intention of buying a hat, but doing something else, entirely?

And if she lied to him about that, what else might she have lied about?

Eventually, he went back to his own hotel to see if she had left any messages for him. Instead, he found her sitting in the lobby, again.

"We need to talk," she said.

"I think we do."

"Can we walk?"

"Why not?"

They went outside and started to walk.

"I went looking for you at the hat shop," he said. "They told me you'd never been there."

"No," she said, "I wasn't."

"So you lied to me?"

"It was a little white lie."

"How many of those have you told me?" he asked.

"I'm sorry," she said, "but I can explain."

"Good," he said, "because I'd like an explanation before I decide to keep helping you."

She stopped walking, turned to face him.

"Can we go and sit somewhere?"

"Sure."

"My room or yours?"

"Neither."

"Then where?"

He looked around, and then pointed,

"There."

She looked at the building he was pointing to, across the street.

"That's a schoolhouse."

"Let's see if school is in session," he suggested.

They crossed to the building. Clint went to the door, opened it and peered inside.

"It's empty," he said. "Let's go in."

They stepped inside and closed the door. Clint looked around at all the small desks, then up to the front at the larger one.

"Let's go over there."

They walked to the front of the room and Olivia sat in the teacher's chair. Clint perched a hip on the teacher's desk, but did it so that he could keep an eye on the front door.

"So," he said, "white lie."

"Yes," she said. "I was going to see someone and I didn't want to tell you."

"Okay," Clint said. "Are you ready to tell me now?"

She hesitated, then said, "Yes."

He waited. When nothing was forth coming, he raised his eyebrows.

"Olivia?"

She took a deep breath.

"I went to see Verna."

"Verna," Clint said. "Why did you go to see her?"

"I needed to talk to her."

"Why?"

Olivia hesitated.

"Olivia," Clint asked, "do you know Verna? I mean, before you came to Winslow, had you known her?"

"No."

"So this was the first time you ever spoke to her?"

"Yes."

"And you did that . . . why?"

Olivia licked her lips, looked away from him and said, "She's my mother."

Chapter Thirty-Three

"You've had a lot if visitors today," Bruno said, when Verna came down to her office. "What was it all about?"

"You know," she said. "That watch everyone's lookin' for."

"Jackson's watch?" Bruno said. "What's so important about it?"

"Who knows?"

"He never told you?"

She sat at her desk and looked up at him.

"No, he didn't."

"What do you think—"

"Bruno, the girls are startin' to come downstairs," she said, cutting him off. "Get out there."

He stiffened as she gave him the order, then said, "Yes, Ma'am," and left.

***

"What?"

"She's my mother."

"Did you know that when you came to town?" he asked.

"Yes."

"How?"

"My father wrote and told me," she explained.

"And that's why you came here?" Clint asked. "To meet her for the first time?"

"Yes."

"But when you got here—"

"My father was in jail, sentenced to be hanged," she said. "That was all I could think about."

"So today you decided to meet her."

"Yes."

At least Clint now knew why Verna had already been awake when he got there.

"So how did it go?"

"I don't know, exactly," Olivia said. "We talked, but only briefly." She shook her head. "I never thought I'd find out my mother was a whore."

"Your father didn't tell you that in his letter?"

"No."

"And you hold that against her?"

"I've always held it against her that she left me and my father when I was a baby."

"And now?" he asked. "Is all forgiven?"

"No," she said, "but now my father's dead, so I only have my mother."

"Does she admit to being your mother?"

"Oh, yes," Olivia said. "No doubt."

"Did you ask her about the watch?"

"I did," Olivia said. "She says she doesn't have it."

"Did you believe her?"

"Why would she lie about it?" Olivia asked.

"Greed?"

"Clint," Olivia said, "she's my mother."

"Who hasn't seen you since you were an infant," Clint pointed out.

"So you think my father gave her the watch and she's not telling me?"

"I'm just saying it's possible."

"Then I should go and ask her again," Olivia said, "except . . ."

"Except what?"

"I don't really want to go back to that house," Olivia said. "The way they looked at me . . . it made me uncomfortable."

"Then get her to come to you," he suggested.

"How do I do that?"

"Send her a message," Clint said. "Ask her to come to your hotel."

"Would you take the message to her?"

"No," he said. "I want to be with you at the hotel when she comes."

"If she comes."

"Did the two of you say everything you need to say?" he asked.

"No, I don't think so."

"Then if she admitted she's your mother," he reasoned, "she'll come."

"So you now believe the watch wasn't stolen by the undertaker?"

"Or the sheriff," he said. "No, I don't. I think your father probably gave it to Verna for safekeeping."

"Victoria," Olivia said.

"What?"

"Her true name is Victoria Jackson," she said. "When she came west, she used Verna."

"Okay," Clint said. "Verna or Victoria, write her a short note asking her to meet you."

"When?" she asked.

"Tomorrow morning," Clint said. "By then we'll be ready for her."

"Ready with what?" Olivia asked.

"The right questions."

Chapter Thirty-Four

They left the schoolhouse just as a teacher was coming down the street leading a string of students, both boys and girls.

"They must've been on an outing," Olivia said.

"Can I help you?" the middle-aged teacher asked, as they reached the schoolhouse.

"No, thank you," Clint said. "We were just leaving."

"But—" the woman said, as Clint and Olivia turned and walked away.

***

Back at Olivia's hotel they went to her room and he watched while she wrote the note to her mother.

"Should it be longer?" she asked.

He read it: PLEASE COME TO MY HOTEL IN THE MORNING SO WE CAN TALK MORE.

"No, this is fine," he said.

"How do we get it to her?"

"I'll talk to the desk clerk and see if he can arrange it."

"And what should I do?"

"I think you should stay here and think about what other little white lies you may have told me."

"But—"

He held up his hand to quiet her and said, "Think it over," and left.

*　*　*

The desk clerk agreed to have the message delivered to Verna's whorehouse without delay.

"Thank you," Clint said, and handed him a dollar.

"Thank *you*, sir."

Clint left the hotel and, once again, had to consider his next move. But there was really nothing to be done until Verna came to Olivia's hotel in the morning. As long as he was convinced that Verna had the watch, there was nothing else for him to do.

He headed back to the Wicker Hotel, but as he approached the front door, he noticed the people on the street stopping and staring—not at him.

He turned to look, and saw a rider coming down the street. The desk clerk of his hotel came and stood next to him.

"Do you know who that is?" he asked the clerk.

"I'm afraid I do, sir," the clerk said. "His name is Red Cantrell."

***

Samuel Kipness looked up from his desk as Sheriff Osborne came bursting through the doors. The lawman didn't stop at his desk, just kept on going right past him toward the Judge's chambers.

"You can't go in th—" Samuel started to shout at Sheriff Osborne.

"Shut up!" Osborne snapped. He barged into the Judge's chambers.

"What's the meaning of this?" Anderson demanded.

"Red Cantrell just rode into town."

Anderson didn't look surprised, but he said, "That was quick."

"Is he comin' here to see you?"

"Why would he be doing that?"

"Because you're the one who sent word about Clint Adams killin' his brother."

"Are you accusing me—"

"I'm just askin' you, Judge," Osborne said. "Did you do that? Is he comin' here to see you before he does anythin'?"

"The answer to your first question is no," Anderson said. "The answer to the second is, how would I know?"

"If he does come to see you, what're you gonna say to him?" the sheriff asked.

"I don't know that, either," Anderson said. "I won't know until it happens—if it does."

"Look Judge—"

"But if Cantrell really is here," the Judge went on, "then you better get out there and do your job, Sheriff. Let him know we won't put up with any . . . shenanigans."

Osborne stared at the Judge for a few moments more, then turned and stalked out.

Judge Anderson sat back in his chair and folded his hands in his lap. This was going to be very interesting.

***

Clint watched as Red Cantrell rode past him without giving him a second look. That might have meant that Cantrell had no idea what he looked like. But he was probably going to talk to somebody to try and find out. It might be the Judge, or the sheriff, or someone who knew both of the Cantrell brothers.

There was no way of telling how quickly Cantrell would then act.

Chapter Thirty-Five

Clint waited at his hotel, seated in the lobby, assuming the Sheriff would come by to see him. He was right.

"Did you see him?" Osborne asked, coming in.

Clint got to his feet.

"I did," he said.

"What're you gonna do?"

"What can I do?" Clint asked. "Wait."

"You're gonna let him make the first move?" Sheriff Osborne asked.

"Why not?" Clint asked. "What if he's not here to make any move at all, but simply to bury his brother?"

"That ain't likely, Adams," Osborne said. "He's here to kill you."

"And you know this . . . how?"

"Well, because . . . he's Red Cantrell!"

Something occurred to Clint, then.

"How well do you know Red Cantrell?" he asked.

"Just to see 'im," Osborne said. "I don't know 'im well. I sure don't know 'im as well as I knew his brother."

"And how well does Judge Anderson know him?"

"That I don't know."

"Don't know, or won't say?"

"I shouldn't say," the lawman said, "since I don't know for sure."

"So you don't know if the Judge is going to send Red after me?"

"God, no," Osborne said. "But why would he have to? I'm tellin' you, Red Cantrell is here to kill you."

"Then as the town sheriff, why don't you warn him not to do that?"

"Um, you want me to tell him—"

"I'm not asking you to run him out of town," Clint said, "just warn him."

"But . . . what would I say?"

"Tell him I'm working for the judge as a special investigator," Clint said. "Make it seem like you're warning him, for his own good."

"I could do that," Osborne said. "I guess."

"Believe me," Clint said, "it would save a lot of trouble."

"I suppose," Osborne said. "But tell me . . . you're not afraid of Red Cantrell, are you?"

"Yes," Clint said.

"You are?"

"Yes," Clint said, "I'm afraid he'll make me kill him, the way his brother did. Believe me, I have no desire to kill brothers."

"Okay," Osborne said, "I'll see what I can do."

"Thank you, Sheriff."

***

Osborne returned to his office, found a message that the Judge wanted to see him. He went to City Hall and presented himself in front of Samuel Kipness's desk.

"So, you're not going to charge right in, this time?" Samuel asked.

"He sent for me," Osborne said.

"I know," Samuel said, "I left the message on your desk. Go on in."

Sheriff Osborne entered the Judge's chambers.

"You wanted to see me, your Honor?"

"You went to Clint Adams' hotel a little while ago," Anderson said.

"How do you know that?"

"I saw you," the Judge said. "I see everything, Sheriff."

"So?" Osborne said. "You want me to keep an eye on him, right?"

"I don't want you warning him about Red Cantrell."

"Cantrell rode into town plain as day, Judge," Osborne said. "I didn't have to warn him."

"So Adams knows Cantrell's in town?"

"Yeah, he does."

"I want you to stay away from both of them."

"Why?"

"Because I want whatever is going to happen to happen," the Judge said. "Have you got that?"

"I got it."

"Just concern yourself with finding that goddamned watch!" Anderson said.

"Yes, sir."

"Now get out."

Osborne turned and stormed out, walking past Samuel's desk without looking at him.

Samuel stood and went into the Judge's chambers.

"What do you want?" Anderson asked.

"You told me to come in when the sheriff left," Samuel said.

"Did I?"

Samuel was worried about Judge Anderson. The man seemed to be forgetting things, lately.

"Yes, sir."

"Why?"

"I—I don't know, sir."

"Well then, get out," Anderson said, "I'm busy."

"Yes, sir."

Samuel went back out to his own desk.

Chapter Thirty-Six

On one hand, Clint thought he should stay in his room until morning, when he would go and meet Olivia at hers. On the other hand, he thought he should go to a saloon and show that he wasn't hiding from Red Cantrell.

Did he want to protect his own ego and not hide from the man, and take a chance on having to kill or be killed before he was done with Olivia's problem? He preferred to finish with one problem before handling another. If, indeed, Red Cantrell was going to be a problem.

He decided his ego could stand it if he remained in his room and read.

***

In the morning he had breakfast in his hotel's dining room, then walked to Olivia's hotel. She opened the door immediately to his knock.

"Oh," she said, "I thought it might be her."

"I'm glad it wasn't," he said. "I wanted to be here."

He closed the door as she walked to the window.

"Do you think she'll come?" she asked.

"You've talked with her already about the subject," he said. "Do you think she's finished with it?"

"No."

"Then she'll come. Have you had breakfast?"

"I went downstairs early and had something," she said, rubbing her hands together. Then she turned to face him. "Do I look all right?"

She was wearing a loose fitting blue dress, which he thought might have had something to do with her mother's profession.

"I mean," she said, before he could answer, "I didn't want to wear anything—you know, too tight. I mean I'm not a—"

"Your mother is not going to judge you by what you wear, Olivia."

"The others did," she said. "All those girls who work for her? They . . . stared at me."

"Maybe they thought you were applying for a job," he said, "and thought you might take theirs."

That made her smile, but she still kept her arms folded, like she was cold.

"What about Red Cantrell?" she asked.

"What about him?"

"When I was eating, I heard talk that he rode into town yesterday."

"That's right, he did."

"Have you seen him?"

"I saw him ride in," Clint said, "but if you're asking if we've talked, no, we haven't."

"Do you think he'll be coming after you?"

"I've asked the sheriff to try to convince him otherwise," Clint said. "I'm hoping he'll bury his brother and then leave town."

"And do you think that's likely?"

"No."

"I'm worried, then," she said. "All the talk I heard said he's the fastest gun . . . well, ever!"

"I guess I might be finding that out for myself," Clint said.

"How can you joke about it?"

"I'm not," Clint said. "The only way I'm going to find out for sure is to go up against him."

"Which you don't want to do."

"Only because I don't want to kill him."

"Or have him kill you," she added.

"Exactly."

The conversation had gone in a direction he had not intended, so he was glad when there was a knock at the door.

***

When Samuel Kipness looked up at his visitor, he thought he recognized him, but had never seen the man before.

"Can I help you?"

"Yeah," the tall, slender man said. "I'd like to see Judge Anderson."

"Can I tell him your name?"

"Red Cantrell."

Samuel got a chill. That was why the stranger seemed familiar. He looked like Wes Cantrell, only older.

"Please wait here."

Samuel rose and knocked on the judge's door.

"What?"

The clerk opened the door, stepped in and closed it.

"What do you want?" the judge demanded. "I told you I was busy."

"He's here!" Samuel hissed.

"Who? Adams?"

"No," Samuel said. "Red Cantrell. He's standing out by my desk."

"Is that a fact?"

"Yes, sir. Should I send for the sheriff?"

"No," Anderson said. "Just tell Cantrell to come in."

"Are you sure—"

"Do it, damn it!"

"Yessir!"

Samuel turned and left the chambers.

Chapter Thirty-Seven

Olivia opened the door and looked at her mother. Verna was wearing a green dress, one considerably tighter than her daughter's.

"Verna," Olivia said. "Please, come in."

It didn't surprise Clint that Olivia didn't call Verna "mother."

Verna walked in, looked surprised to see Clint there.

"Good-morning, Verna," he said.

"Mr. Adams." She turned to Olivia. "Why is he here?"

"He wanted to talk to you."

She turned back to Clint. "About?"

"The watch."

"Again?"

"Nobody has it," Clint said. "Nobody stole it. Victor gave it to somebody for safekeeping."

"So?"

"So the only person in this town he would've given it to would be you."

"Look," Verna said "I told you—"

"I know what you told me, Verna," Clint said. "You had it, and somebody stole it from your room."

"Right."

"Not sure I believe that."

Verna looked at Olivia.

"Why would I lie?" she asked.

Olivia looked at Clint.

"Apparently," Clint said, "there's a lot of money involved. Or something worth a lot of money."

"And you think I'm trying to keep it for myself?" she asked. "To cheat my own daughter?"

"A daughter you only just met," Clint said. "You two don't even know each other."

"So I'm just a thief."

"Verna, look—"

"No, you look," Verna said. "Both of you. I don't know how Victor found me here. And since he's dead, I'll never know. But I left him years ago because I didn't want to be a wife, and I didn't want to be a mother." She looked at Olivia. "I'm sorry, but it's true. I would've been a horrible mother. And I guess I'm provin' that, now."

She turned and stormed out of the room.

"I guess she is," Olivia said.

"I've got to go," Clint said.

"Why?"

"I just thought of something, and I need to talk to the sheriff about it. Will you be all right?"

"Sure," she said, "it's not like I thought she was going to welcome me with open arms."

"I'm going to find that watch, Olivia," he said. "Count on it."

He left the room.

***

"Take a seat, Red," Judge Anderson said.

"I ain't here to sit," Red Cantrell said. "Whataya want, Judge?"

"Just wanted to give you my condolences on the death of your brother."

"Wes didn't die, he was shot and killed by Clint Adams," Red Cantrell said. "Where is he?"

"He's in town, somewhere," the judge answered. "What do you intend to do, Red?"

"I'm gonna bury my brother, and then kill Adams," Cantrell said. "What would you expect me to do?"

"Exactly that," Anderson said. "I just wanted to be sure."

"Just make sure your lawman doesn't try to get in my way," Red Cantrell said. "Unless you wanna lose him, too."

"I'll keep that in mind, Red."

"You do that," Cantrell said. "And maybe I won't burn this whole town down while I'm at it."

Cantrell turned and left.

***

It occurred to Clint that Victor Jackson had not been executed for stealing a horse and killing the owner. He had been hanged because somebody wanted that watch, and whatever treasure it was supposed to lead to. The horse and its owner had been sacrificed.

He tried the sheriff's office first, but Osborne wasn't there. He had to find Osborne, as he was the only one who could answer his questions—if the lawman would even answer them honestly.

Unless . . .

***

As he entered the saloon, he saw Bill Jellicoe cleaning the bar top, since there was nobody bellied up to it, at that moment.

"You're here pretty early," Jelly said. "Will it be beer or coffee?"

"Coffee, thanks."

"Comin' up."

Jelly went and poured two cups, came over and pushed one across the bar to Clint.

"What brings you out so early?" Jelly asked. "Is it Annie?"

"No," Clint said. "She's a nice kid, but no. I wanted to talk to you, Jelly."

"Me?" The bartender leaned his elbows on the bar. "You wanna ask for her hand?"

"Again," Clint said, "she's a nice kid, but no. I want to hear what you know about the man who Victor Jackson supposedly killed."

"Supposedly?" Jelly asked, shrugging. "After all, he hung for it."

"I know. But do you think he did it?"

"I can't tell you," Jelly said. "I didn't know Victor Jackson."

"Did you know the victim?"

"Dizzy Randall? Oh, yeah, sure, everybody in town knew him."

"How?"

"He was the town drunk."

Chapter Thirty-Eight

"The town drunk?"

"Oh, yeah," Jelly said. "Fell down in here and spent the night lots of times."

"They said that Victor Jackson tried to steal this man's horse, and ended up killing him. How does that sound to you?"

"Odd," Jelly said, "I have to admit."

"Why?"

"I never knew Dizzy to own anythin', let alone a horse."

"That's what I thought," Clint said. He drank half his coffee, put the cup down. "Thanks for the coffee."

Clint left the saloon and, again, went looking for Sheriff Osborne.

***

This time when he entered the sheriff's office the man was there, seated at his desk, looking unhappy.

"You look like you just lost your best friend," Clint said. "Did you talk to Red Cantrell, yet?"

"No," Osborne said. "The judge gave me a tongue lashin'."

"About what?"

"Stayin' out of Red Cantrell's business with you," the lawman explained.

"I thought he'd feel that way," Clint said, "but that's not why I'm here."

"Then why?"

"Dizzy Randall," Clint said.

"What about him?" Osborne asked. "He's dead."

"I just found out he was the town drunk."

"So?"

"So how would the town drunk have a horse that somebody would want to steal?"

"I don't know."

"The whole thing sounds off to me, Sheriff," Clint said. "Like a set up excuse to execute Victor Jackson and get him out of the way."

"For what reason?"

"What else? That watch."

"You're crazy."

"You arrested Jackson, right?"

"That's right."

"Why? What led you to him?"

"A witness."

"And who was this witness?"

"Just a man passin' by," Osborne said. "A stranger, which is why it wouldn't have made sense to call him a liar."

"And where is this stranger now?"

"He left town right after the trial."

"That's convenient."

"What are you sayin', Adams?"

"That somebody framed Victor Jackson for the killing," Clint said.

"You mean you think somebody else killed Dizzy?"

"That never occurred to you?"

"Not once the witness came to me," Osborne admitted. "So now you're not only looking for the watch, but for a new killer?"

"That's about it," Clint said.

"But what good would it do now?"

"It would clear Jackson's name for his daughter," Clint said, "And put the real killer behind bars, or worse."

"But the Judge would have to admit he made a mistake," the lawman said.

"That's right," Clint said, "he was judge *and* jury."

"That man has never admitted to bein' wrong," Osborne pointed out.

"Maybe he wasn't wrong," Clint said.

"Meanin'?"

"Meaning he knew all along that Victor Jackson was innocent," Clint said.

Chapter Thirty-Nine

Instead of solving the mystery of the watch, Clint had unearthed a new mystery to solve—who actually killed the town drunk? And what he really wanted to know was if Judge Anderson was behind the whole thing.

On the other hand, he was having thoughts about Verna that he hadn't had before. After Victor Jackson gave her the watch to keep safe, would she have orchestrated his execution so she could keep it? That was something he was going to have to figure out. After all, she wouldn't have killed Dizzy Randall on her own, she would've needed help from somebody like Bruno, who just happened to be in love with her.

But as he left the sheriff's office, he knew Osborne was not going to have the gumption to warn Red Cantrell off, so he would have to keep looking over his shoulder for the gunman. Unless he took hold of the reins of the situation and went at it head on.

***

"I can't do that," Abner Weatherly said to Red Cantrell. "I have to bury another man tomorrow, the one they hanged."

"Now, I got somethin' I gotta do, undertaker, and I ain't gonna do it 'til my brother is buried. You bury Wes tomorrow mornin', and I'll pay you double. Then you can bury that other fella any time."

"Double?"

"I can either pay you double," Cantrell said, "or kill ya right now and bury him myself in one of your boxes. It's your call."

"Um," Weatherly said, "I guess I'll bury him in the mornin'."

"Smart man," Cantrell said, and pressed the money into Weatherly's hand.

***

Clint stopped in front of the undertaker's place. Through the window he could see two men talking, Weatherly, and a tall, thin man he recognized as Red Cantrell. He decided to go across the street and wait for Cantrell to leave.

After about ten minutes, the gunman came out and walked off down the street. Clint crossed over and entered the undertaker's establishment.

"If you're gonna threaten me," Weatherly said, "I've already been threatened."

"Not what I had in mind."

"Then what?"

"What did Cantrell want?"

"He wants me to bury his brother so he can kill you," Weatherly said.

"He said that?"

"He said he wants me to bury Wes tomorrow because he has somethin' he has to do, and can't do it until his brother is buried." Weatherly shrugged. "What else does he have to do?"

"Can you bury him tomorrow?"

"I was going to bury Mr. Jackson tomorrow mornin'," Weatherly said. "Then Wes the next day. I'll have to switch 'em."

"How would Jackson's daughter feel about that?" Clint asked.

"I don't know," Weatherly said. "But I'm not willing to die just to satisfy her." Suddenly, the undertaker looked like he got an idea. "Maybe if you killed him before tomorrow?"

"I'm not going to do that as a favor to you, Mr. Weatherly."

"He's gonna come after you," Weatherly said. "To-morrow, or today, what's the difference?"

"There's a difference to me," Clint said. "What if you don't bury Wes tomorrow?"

"Red will kill me."

"Just for putting it off one day?"

"Yes."

"Mr. Weatherly," Clint said, "did you steal that man's watch?"

Weatherly stared at Clint.

"I didn't."

"Have you ever stolen anything from a dead body?" Clint asked.

Weatherly licked his lips.

"I may have, but not this time," Weatherly said.

"So who did?" Clint asked. "The Judge? The Sheriff?"

Weatherly frowned.

"What're you tryin' to pull?" Weatherly asked.

"I think you were all after this watch," Clint said, "but none of you have it."

Weatherly looked very interested.

"Then where is it?" he asked. "Who has it?"

"Abner," Clint said, "can you tell me what's in the watch?"

"If I do," Weatherly said, "I'm dead."

Abner Weatherly's desire for self-preservation was strong.

"You're gonna have to find that out for yourself," he told Clint. "And I'm burying Wes Cantrell in the mornin'."

"Okay," Clint said. "And I'll be there."

"What?"

"I'll watch you bury him," Clint said. "After all, I killed him."

"What do you think Red's gonna do if you show up at the graveyard?" Weatherly asked.

"I guess we're going to find out."

"If you two start shootin'—"

"You worried you might get hit by a stray shot?" Clint asked.

"Well . . . yeah."

"Don't worry," Clint said, "between me and Red Cantrell, there won't be any stray shots."

"Still," Weatherly said, "if you kill him today—"

"Forget that," Clint said. "Today I need to find that watch. Tomorrow I have to deal with Red."

Clint started for the door.

"Adams!"

He turned.

"The Judge, he wanted that watch real bad," Weatherly said. "He made me and the sheriff . . . but I thought Osborne had it, and he thought I had it."

"So none of you have it."

"No."

Clint nodded.

"Okay, thanks, Abner."

He left, now certain that Verna had the watch. But had she taken steps to get rid of Victor Jackson in order to keep it?

Chapter Forty

Clint banged his fist on the door of the whorehouse.

"You again?" Bruno demanded.

"I need to see Verna," Clint said.

"She doesn't wanna see you," Bruno said.

"Just tell her—"

"No," Bruno said, putting his huge hand against Clint's chest. "She said she doesn't wanna see you no more."

Clint took a step back.

"Tell me, Bruno," Clint said, "did you kill Dizzy Randall and frame Victor Jackson? Did you do that for Verna?"

"You're crazy," the bouncer said.

"If you did, I'll find out and prove it," Clint said.

"They already hung a man for killin' Dizzy," Bruno said. "Now don't come back here, Adams, or I just might have to break your back."

Bruno slammed the door in Clint's face.

***

Clint found out there was only one doctor in town. His name was Doc Lennox, and he had an office on a side street, above a leather store. He found it, went up the stairs and knocked on the locked door. The man who answered was older, small, and moved very slowly.

"Yes?"

"Are you Doc Lennox."

"Yes, I am. Are you sick? Injured?"

"No, I just need to ask you some questions."

"About what?"

"Dizzy Randall."

Doc Lennox frowned.

"Come in."

"I'm sorry if I'm interrupting—"

"I don't have a patient now," the doctor said. "I was just having a sandwich." He walked to his desk, where half a sandwich was waiting. "Do you mind?"

"No, that's fine," Clint said. "Keep eating."

Doc Lennox took a bite, then asked, "What can I do for you?"

"Were you the doctor who pronounced Dizzy Randall dead?" Clint asked.

"Since I'm the only doctor in town, the answer to that is, yes."

"What did he die of?"

Lennox chewed, swallowed and said, "A broken back."

"Thank you, Doctor."

"Is that all?" Doc Lennox asked, but Clint was already out the door.

***

"Osborne!"

The sheriff turned, saw Clint running up to him on the street.

"Adams."

"I checked your office," Clint said, "then started looking all over town for you."

"And here I am," Osborne said. "What is it? Is this about Red Cantrell?"

"No," Clint said, "Red's not going to do anything until tomorrow."

"And why's that?"

"That's when he's burying his brother," Clint said. "And he says he's got something to do after he buries him."

"Kill you?"

"Seems likely," Clint said. "But I'm not here about Red. I'm here to talk to you about some other things."

"Like what?"

"The bouncer at the whorehouse," Clint said. "Bruno, and Verna, and a watch."

Chapter Forty-One

Osborne agreed to go to a saloon with Clint for the talk. Clint chose to take him to the Holloway House Saloon, attached to the hotel, where they each sat over a beer. That way if they accomplished anything, he could just go upstairs and tell Olivia.

"So you want me to believe that Verna had Bruno break Dizzy Randall's back and framed Jackson?"

"Yes," Clint said, "that's what I want you to believe."

"Why?"

"Okay," Clint said. "Verna is Olivia Jackson's mother."

"She was married to Jackson?" Osborne asked, in shock.

"No, but she did have a baby with him, and then left and came west."

"So what were the three of them doin' in Winslow?"

"I'm not sure how Jackson knew Verna was here," Clint said. "We may never know that, but Jackson sent for Olivia, telling her about Verna in a letter."

"And by the time she got here, he'd been convicted and hanged."

"Yes."

"What about Weatherly?" Osborne asked. "You don't suspect him, anymore?"

"Not of stealing the watch," Clint said. "And I don't suspect you anymore, either."

"And the Judge?"

"He had something to do with it," Clint said. "And he's still looking for the watch, isn't he?"

"Yeah, he is."

"Maybe he and Verna are in it together," Clint said. "Has the Judge ever been to the whorehouse?"

"He's an old man!"

"That doesn't mean he can't watch," Clint said.

"Jesus . . ." Osborne shook his head.

"I just wanted you to know I'm going after Verna, Bruno, and probably the Judge."

"And you're gonna do this today?" Osborne asked, "So you can deal with Red Cantrell tomorrow."

"That's right."

"And where are you gonna do that?"

"At the graveyard, tomorrow morning," Clint said. "I'm going to watch them bury Wes."

"Jesus," Osborne said. "Red'll kill you as soon as the last shovelful of dirt hits that box."

"That'll be better than some innocent bystander getting hit by a stray shot."

"Between you and Red Cantrell," Osborne said, "there shouldn't be any stray shots."

"That's what I said to Mr. Weatherly," Clint said. "But I really don't know how good Red Cantrell is. Do you?"

"I've seen him once or twice," Osborne said. "He's fast, Adams. Real fast."

"It's going to come down to who's the most accurate."

"Oh, Red's accurate," the lawman said.

Clint finished his beer.

"When we're done here," he said, "you can go straight to the Judge."

"Is that what this was about?"

"I wouldn't want to get you in trouble, Sheriff," Clint said, seeing someone come through the batwing doors. "Go ahead and tell him I'm coming for him."

"Adams—"

"Or not," Clint said, standing. "It's up to you."

"No, Adams," Osborne said, "Red Cantrell just came into the saloon."

"I know," Clint said. "That's why I stood up."

Red Cantrell approached the table, stopped a few feet away. Conversation in the saloon died down, and then chairs began to scrape the floor as the others in the saloon moved away, giving them room.

"Sheriff," Cantrell said, looking at Clint.

"Red," Osborne said, "not here—"

"Relax," Cantrell said. "I'm here to talk to Mr. Adams."

"Really?" Clint said. "Go ahead, talk."

Red looked at Osborne.

"Don't you have somethin' to do, Sheriff?" the gunman asked.

"Sure," Osborne said, standing up. "Just talk, right?"

"That's it," Red said. "I have to bury my brother tomorrow."

"Right," Osborne said, and left.

"Shall we sit?" Clint asked.

"Sure."

A girl came over to the table and Red Cantrell said, "Two beers."

"Yes, sir."

"On me," the gunman said, to Clint.

"Thanks."

"There's no reason two men who are gonna try to kill each other can't have a beer together."

The girl came back with the beers, set them down and hurried away. The saloon remained silent. Some customers had decided to leave, others stayed to watch, from a distance.

Chapter Forty-Two

"I'm sorry," Clint said.

"What?"

"He gave me no choice, forced the issue," Clint said. "He was a bad poker player."

"I know," Red said, "and a poor loser."

"You know that?"

"He was my brother," Red said. "I knew everythin' about him."

"So what do you plan to do after you bury him tomorrow?" Clint asked.

"Oh," Red said, "I'm gonna kill you."

"Even though you know what kind of man he was?"

"He was still my brother," Red Cantrell said. "And it won't do my reputation any harm to kill the Gunsmith."

Clint studied the man. He looked to be in his late thirties, making him at least ten years older than his brother was.

"Cantrell—"

"You can call me Red," Cantrell said. "After all, we're gonna try to kill each other . . . Clint."

"Well, Red," Clint said, "you're not what I expected."

"What did you expect?"

"To be honest," Clint said, "a soulless killer."

"I'm a killer," Cantrell said, "you got that part right. But I kill for a reason, and this time the reason is family."

He drank his beer, set the empty mug down, and stood up.

"I'll be buryin' my brother in the mornin'," Red said. "After that—"

"Don't worry," Clint said, "I'll be there. I killed him, I'll watch you bury him."

"Good," Cantrell said. "That'll make it easier. I'll see you then."

"Thanks for the beer," Clint said.

Red Cantrell nodded, and left the saloon.

Clint sat for a while, drinking his beer while the others in the room went back to their tables and began to talk amongst themselves again.

He was going to have to try to settle this whole watch business tonight, because when he faced Red Cantrell, he didn't want to have anything else on his mind.

He finished his beer and left the Holloway House without stopping first to see Olivia.

***

He knew he was going to have to deal with Verna and Bruno again. There was no getting around it. He went back to the whorehouse, determined to face Verna openly with his accusations. That would mean getting past Bruno.

But he didn't have to knock on the door. It was business hours, and it was unlocked, so he walked in.

"Hello, handsome," a blonde girl called out to him. She came running over, took hold of his left arm. "Blonde, brunette or redhead? Or somethin' more exotic?"

"None, I'm afraid," Clint said. "I'm here to see the lady of the house."

"Oh honey," she said, "we're all ladies, here."

"I mean Verna."

"Oh, the boss lady," she said. "I'm afraid you have to talk to Bruno first."

"Yeah, I'd like to avoid that if I can."

"Why?" she asked. "Are you afraid of him? I mean, he's pretty big, but you look like you can take care of yourself."

"I'm afraid I might have to shoot him."

"I'd like to see that," she said. She removed her arm from his. "If you stay put, I'll tell Verna you're here." She started to walk away, then stopped and turned. "What's your name?"

"Clint Adams."

She stared at him, said, "Oh," and walked away.

***

When Sheriff Osborne left Clint at the saloon, he walked to City Hall, with the intention of doing what Clint told him to do, talk to Judge Anderson. But when he got to the front door, he had second thoughts. He decided to let it go and see what happened.

He turned and went to his office.

***

Several other girls approached him while he waited, and he rejected them as gently as he could. When the girl came back she said, "Come with me." She was not the least bit flirtatious, as he had been when he got there.

"What's your name?" he asked.

"I'm Denise."

"Denise, are you taking me to Verna, or Bruno?"

Her eyes shifted and she said, "Verna."

"Good," he said. "Lead the way."

Chapter Forty-Three

Denise led him to a door. It wasn't the door to Verna's office.

"You can go in," she said.

"Without you?"

"Um, I was told not to," she said, and scurried away down the hall.

Clint looked at the door, pressed his ear to it. He was still on the first floor. Further down the hall he saw another door, had a feeling it led outside. He walked to it, opened it and saw that he was right. Stepping out, he found himself behind the building. He walked around to the side, figured out which window went with the door Denise had taken him to.

He moved to the window, stood to one side and peered in. Bruno was standing by the door, waiting. He had no weapon in his hands. Clint couldn't see the entire room, so he didn't know if Verna was there.

He thought about breaking the window, but he didn't want to attract a lot of attention from inside the building. So he returned to the back door and went down the hall to the door. He put his hand on it, felt that it was not particularly solid. He set his back against the opposite wall, then lashed out with his foot, kicking the door open.

There was a yell from inside as the door slammed into Bruno. Clint sprang through the open doorway with his gun in his hand. He ducked to the left, turned and pointed the gun at Bruno, who came out from behind the door.

"Stay right there, Bruno."

"You ain't gonna shoot me," the big man said. "I ain't armed."

"Don't push me," Clint said. "Tell me about Dizzy Randall, Victor Jackson, and the watch."

"Naw," Bruno said, "I think I'll break your back, instead."

"The way you broke Dizzy's back?" Clint asked. "If you're going to keep killing people, Bruno, you better find a different way of doing it."

"If I kill any more people, you won't be around to see it, Adams."

"Again," Clint said, "don't make me shoot you."

"You won't kill an unarmed man."

"You're right," Clint said, and shot the big man in the right knee. "But I'll shoot one."

"Ow!" Bruno screamed, falling to the floor and grabbing his knee. "You shot me!"

"I said I would," Clint replied. "Now tell me about Dizzy and the watch, or I'm going to shoot you in the other knee."

At that point, he heard people in the hall, stepped out and said to the men and women there, "Nothing to see here, folks. Go back to your fun."

The people turned and went back up the hall. He noticed Verna wasn't among them.

He stepped back inside, where Bruno was frantically trying to staunch the flow of blood from his shattered knee.

"Jesus," he said, his face etched with pain, "I need a doctor."

"Not yet," Clint said. "I still have to shatter your other knee."

"No!" Bruno held a bloody hand out to Clint. "I—I killed Dizzy because Verna told me to."

"And?"

"And framed Jackson."

"How?"

"By payin' off the witness."

"And then making him leave town."

"Yes," Bruno said, gritting his teeth. "Jeez, this hurts."

"Where's Verna?" Clint asked.

"She has another house at the south end of town," Bruno said. "A small one. She goes there to get away from here."

"And that's where she is now?"

"Yes."

"And she has the watch there?"

Bruno gritted his teeth, then said, "Yes. Come on, Adams! I need a doctor."

"I'll have one of the girls send for Doc Lennox," Clint said, "but he's kind of old and frail. It might take him some time to get here."

He went out the door, left the bleeding man crying on the floor.

***

Judge Jedediah Anderson had a revelation.

He was sitting in his favorite chair in his house with a glass of his favorite wine when it hit him. And he felt no one could handle this situation the way he could. He finished the wine, rose and left his house to walk to the south end of town.

***

At the south end Clint found several small houses, located outside the town limits. Only one looked lived in, with repairs having been done to the outside. This had to be the house Bruno was talking about. Clint doubted the man had the courage to lie in the face of the pain he was suffering.

He approached the front of the house with the idea of knocking, but then decided against it, given what had happened at the whorehouse. Instead, he moved around to one side and started peering in windows.

The first person he saw was Judge Jedediah Anderson.

Chapter Forty-Four

When Verna opened the door, she expected to see Bruno. Nobody else would dare come to her house, and she was waiting for his report on what happened with Clint Adams. She was shocked to see Judge Anderson standing there.

"Jedediah," she said, "what brings you here?"

"I think you know, Verna," he said. "Will you ask me in?"

"Will you come in, Judge?" she invited.

"Thank you."

He entered and she closed the door, ushering him into the small confines of the house.

"I've never been here before," he said. "Very tasteful."

"What do you want, Judge?"

He turned and looked at her. She was wearing a fuzzy, comfortable looking robe, very different from what she wore in her whorehouse.

"How old are you now, Verna? Fifty?" he asked. "You're still a handsome woman."

"Is that why you came here, Judge?" she asked. "To sleep with me. Are you even . . . capable of it, at your age?"

"Let's get right down to it, Verna," the Judge said. "I want that watch."

"Ah."

"We agreed we'd share the treasure," he said, "but you've been avoiding me, claiming the watch was stolen. I don't believe you. You have the watch. I want it."

"Or what, Judge?"

"I'll shut you down, Verna," Judge Anderson said, "and find a reason to jail you. And Bruno, since he actually killed Dizzy Randall."

"Judge—" she started, but then there was another knock on her door.

***

Anderson was standing in the center of the room, talking to Verna. When Clint saw the Judge through the window, he knew tonight would be the night they would put this matter to rest.

The simplest approach would be the best, so he walked to the front door and knocked. When Verna opened the door, she looked surprised.

"Did you think it would be Bruno?" he asked. "Sorry, he's not coming."

"Did you kill him?"

"No," Clint said, "but he doesn't have a leg to stand on."

She closed her eyes.

"Ask me in, Verna," Clint said. "Let's not keep the Judge waiting."

"You might as well come in, then."

As Clint and Verna approached, the Judge looked annoyed.

"What's he doing here?"

"I didn't invite him."

"Adams—" the Judge started.

"Save it, Judge," Clint said. "She had her man Bruno try to kill me tonight. She has the watch. You know it, and I know it."

Both men stared at her. They were both surprised when she took a small derringer from the right hand pocket of her fuzzy, comfortable robe.

"You were expecting Bruno tonight," Clint said. "I assume you were going to shoot him to get him out of the way?"

"Him, you, what's the difference?"

"You bitch—" the Judge said.

"Takes a real bastard to know a bitch, Judge," Verna said.

"So what now, Verna?" Clint asked. "Kill the Judge and me now that you have the watch?"

"First, I'll need you to drop your gun to the floor, Clint," she instructed, ignoring his questions.

"Afraid I can't do that, Verna," Clint said.

"Shoot her," the Judge said. "You're the Gunsmith. Draw and shoot her."

"Shut up, Judge," Clint said. "Or I'll let her shoot you, first."

"You can't—"

Verna pointed the derringer at the judge and pulled the trigger. As the bullet struck the man, he looked shocked, like he had been stung more than shot.

"Bitch—" he said, again, but she cut him off a second time by firing again. This time when the bullet hit him, he folded up and slumped to the floor.

She turned the gun toward Clint.

"Drop your gun," she said. "You can see I'm serious."

"I'm serious too, Verna," he said, "and you've fired both shots from that two shot derringer."

She stared down at the judge, then looked at the derringer in dismay. She pulled the trigger twice, just to be sure, then said, "Oh, shit," in disgust.

"You let him get to you and fired both your shots," Clint said. "So now let's talk about the watch."

"Clint—"

"Don't offer to split with me, Verna," he said. "I'm not interested in whatever treasure the watch leads to. I just want to give it to Olivia."

She nodded, tossed her gun onto the floor, then took her left hand out of her pocket and handed him the watch.

Chapter Forty-Five

"Where did you get it?" Olivia asked, looking at the watch Clint had just put into her hand.

"Verna had it," he said. "I'm sorry, I know she's your mother—"

"I have my doubts about her," she admitted.

"Why is that?" he asked. "Didn't your father tell you who she was?"

"He put it in a letter, but I never had a chance to talk to him about it," she said.

"Well then . . ." he said, and went on to tell her about Verna having Bruno kill Dizzy Randall and frame her father.

"There you are," she said, when he was done. "Would a woman frame her child's father for murder, and then try to cheat her daughter?"

"You'd think not," he said.

She sat down on the bed and looked at the watch in her hand.

"Aren't you going to open it?" he asked.

She rubbed the scarred outside of the formerly gold watch with her fingertips.

"Not yet," she said. "I think I'll just enjoy having it for a while."

"I've got to go over to the sheriff's office," Clint said. "Let's talk in the morning."

"Okay," she said, still stroking the watch.

***

"Oh, good," Osborne said, as Clint entered his office. "I didn't think you'd come back."

"I said I would," Clint reminded him. "I just had to give Olivia her father's watch."

Osborne didn't look happy as he sat behind his desk.

"What's wrong?"

"I've got Verna in a cell and Bruno at the Doc's," the lawman said.

"And?"

"And the judge is at the undertaker's."

"Which part of all that is bad news?" Clint asked. "Verna shot the judge. They both got an innocent man hanged."

"And will another judge take your word for that?" Osborne asked.

"Just question Verna, and Bruno," Clint said. "One of them will talk."

Osborne sat back.

"Actually," he said, "this is not bad news."

"It was bad for Victor Jackson and his daughter."

"And Verna?" the lawman asked. "Is she really this girl's mother?"

"I don't think we'll ever know. Can I go?"

"I don't see why not," Osborne said. "You didn't shoot anybody, this time. I'll need a written statement from you in the mornin'."

"You'll get it."

"Preferably," Osborne added, as Clint headed for the door, "before Red Cantrell kills you."

***

Clint went back to Olivia's hotel and knocked on her door.

"Have you opened it, yet?" he asked, as she admitted him.

"No," she said, "I thought I'd wait for you."

She walked to the table by the bed and picked up the watch, then joined him by the foot of the bed.

"Well," he said, "this is what we've been waiting for."

She nodded and opened the pocket watch.

There was nothing in it but the face of the watch.

"Verna must've taken it," Olivia said.

"Taken what?"

"The map," Olivia said. "Didn't you think there'd be a map inside?"

"Well, yeah," Clint said, "but what are those scratch-es?"

Olivia examined at the cover of the watch, which seemed to have something scratched into it on the inside.

"Oh my," Olivia said. "Is that . . . could that be a map?"

"Could be," Clint said, "a miniature map."

"But . . . how do I know what it is? I mean, where it is?"

"Your father came here," Clint said, "so it must depict an area around here. You'll have to find the starting point."

"Do you think we can do that?" she asked.

"We?"

"Well . . . yeah, don't you want to find whatever it leads to?"

"Uh, well, no," Clint said, "I don't. Whatever it is, it's yours."

"But . . . I'll split it with you."

"Olivia . . . no."

"Why not?"

"I only got involved to help you find the watch," he said. "I ended up killing a man, and I may have to kill another one. I'm done."

"You're still going to see Red Cantrell tomorrow?" she asked.

"At his brother's grave," he said, "yeah."

"But he might kill you."

"We've been over this," Clint said. "One way or another this all comes to an end tomorrow . . . for me."

"Clint . . ."

"I'm sorry," he said. "I just don't want to be involved, anymore."

"But then how—"

"I'm sure someone here in town will want to help you," he said. "In fact, try Sheriff Osborne."

"Him?"

"Yeah," Clint said, "I think he's kind of turning over a new leaf. In fact, I have to see him one more time, in the morning. I can mention it."

"Oh, um, well, all right," she said. "Have him come and see me, then."

"Like I said," Clint replied, "I'll mention it to him. You might even consider one more person."

"Verna," Clint said. "She's in jail, and she'll probably be there a long time. Maybe she'll tell you where to start."

"Do you really think so?"

"I don't know," Clint said, "but it's worth a try."

Chapter Forty-Six

Clint checked out of the hotel the next morning, retrieved Eclipse from the livery, and stopped at the sheriff's office. He gave Osborne a written statement, told him that if they needed him to appear at a trial, they could send a telegram to Labyrinth, Texas.

"I've got your statement, and as you said, Verna or Bruno are gonna talk. Should be okay."

"One other thing," Clint said. "Olivia's going to need help with that watch."

Osborne looked interested.

"Was there a map inside?" he asked. "That's what everybody seemed to be thinkin'."

"Nothing on paper, but something is scratched into the inside of the cover. She's going to need help reading it."

"You askin' me?"

"Well, you could let her talk to Verna to try and identify the map, but then yeah, she's going to need help. You might want to think about it, maybe stop by the hotel."

"I'll consider it," Osborne said. "Where are you headed now? Boot hill?"

"That's right."

"Do I need to come along?"

"No," Clint said, "you can just check later, see if one of us is lying up there. You'll know what happened."

"You could ride out of town the other way, you know."

"Yeah," Clint said, walking to the door, "I know."

***

When he got to boot hill, he saw Abner Weatherly standing there while two men dumped dirt down into a grave. Red Cantrell was standing by, with a man wearing a collar.

"Sorry I'm late," Clint said, as he approached.

"No problem," Red said. "Thanks, Father."

"You have my sympathies, my son," the fiftyish priest said. He looked at Clint. "Are you family?"

"No."

"He's just a friend of the family."

The priest nodded, turned and walked away.

The two gravediggers finished filling the dirt back in and walked away with their shovels. That left Clint, Weatherly, and Red Cantrell.

Clint looked at the wooden headstone, on which was written WES CANTRELL and nothing else.

"No birth date?" Clint asked.

"I don't remember it," Red said.

"I gotta go," Weatherly told them.

"No, stay," Red said. "Stand over there and watch. We need a witness that this was on the up-and-up, a fair fight. I don't want the law comin' after me. Plus, you're gonna need to call them gravediggers back with their shovels."

Weatherly nodded and backed away with a worried look on his face.

"You still want to do this?" Clint asked.

"Don't you?" Red asked. "I mean, you coulda rode out of town and not looked back."

"You would've come looking for me," Clint said. "I'm only here to get it done, one way or another."

"And your other business in town?"

"Done."

"So let's do this, then," Red Cantrell said.

They eyed each other across the freshly dug grave. No more talk. Red drew, and he was fast—possibly one of the fastest Clint had ever seen. Accurate wasn't going to do it, this time. He had to actually beat the man to the draw.

As Red's gun cleared leather and started to come up Clint drew and fired. Cantrell's eyes went blank as the bullet hit him and he fell forward onto his brother's grave.

"Jesus," Weatherly said, "he was the fastest gun around."

"Right," Clint said, ejecting his spent shell, replacing it and holstering his gun, "Was. You better dig another hole."

"Who's gonna pay for the box and the headstone?"

"Take the money for the coffin out of what you stole," Clint said, "and just add Red's name by his brother's."

He walked back down to where he had left Eclipse, mounted up, and rode out of Winslow, Arizona.

Coming December 27, 2019

THE GUNSMITH
454
Into the Fire

**For more information
visit:** www.SpeakingVolumes.us

On Sale Now!

THE GUNSMITH *series*
Books 430 - 451

**For more information
visit:** www.SpeakingVolumes.us

Coming December 15, 2019

Lady Gunsmith
8
Roxy Doyle and the Silver Queen

For more information
visit: www.SpeakingVolumes.us

On Sale Now!

Lady Gunsmith 7
Roxy Doyle and the James Boys

For more information
visit:

On Sale Now!

Lady Gunsmith *series*
Books 1-6

For more information
visit: www.SpeakingVolumes.us

On Sale Now!

ANGEL EYES *series*
by Award-Winning Author
Robert J. Randisi (J.R. Roberts)

For more information
visit:

On Sale Now!

TRACKER *series*
by Award-Winning Author
Robert J. Randisi (J.R. Roberts)

On Sale Now!

MOUNTAIN JACK PIKE *series*
by Award-Winning Author
Robert J. Randisi (J.R. Roberts)

For more information
visit: www.SpeakingVolumes.us

Sign up for free and bargain books

Join the Speaking Volumes mailing list

Text

ILOVEBOOKS

to 22828 to get started.